BRING A COWBOY HOME

GLORIA DOTY

It's never too late for love,

Gloria Doty

Cover Design by Gwen Gades
Edited by Nina Newton

ISBN 978-1533326171

Library of Congress Control Number: 2016931569

ACKNOWLEDGMENTS

I consulted many friends and acquaintances who had the expertise I needed to make certain my facts for this novel were indeed plausible.

They were all very gracious about sharing knowledge in their particular field. I want to say thank you to each of them. I was amazed at the amount of people I know who 'know stuff."

Firearms:	Todd Radke
Horses:	Diane Butler Radke
Police Procedure:	Jim Herman
Small Aircraft:	Joel Nichols
Poker:	Chad Taylor / Kevin Leininger
Medical Issues:	Kathy Sias-Head
Towns/Highways in Texas	Kari Shockley

I also want to thank my amazing TEAM at Vox Dei:

Nina Newton, Editor
Gwen Gades, Cover Designer
Pat Spence, Proofreader

AND...the two people who patiently answered a thousand questions:

Heather Huffman, Marketing Manager
Becki Brannen, Project Manager

This book is dedicated to the person who inspired the title many years ago...my good friend, Sherry Hesting. Many years ago, I was preparing to fly to Houston, Texas, to visit my daughter and her family. At that time, Sherry lived in Indianapolis, Indiana. I spent the night at her house, and she took me to the Indianapolis Airport the next morning in time for my flight. As I was about to board the plane, she called out to me, "Bring a cowboy home."

Those words became the basis for this book. Years later, Sherry lost her battle with breast cancer, but I would always treasure her friendship and her words of advice.

CHAPTER 1

PHOEBE DROPPED LUCY and her bag at O'Hare's curbside check-in. As she drove off, Lucy heard her shouting, "Don't forget. Bring a cowboy home this time!"

Lucy smiled and shook her head at her friend's never-ending quest to find her a man and subsequent romance.

"Sure thing," she muttered to no one in particular.

The slightly stooped man checking her bag obviously heard the exchange. He smiled at her. "You may need a bigger bag on your return flight if your cowboy is bringing his horse home, too."

Lucy rolled her eyes and laughed out loud. "I'll let him buy the ticket for his horse."

"Good idea."

Chicago's O'Hare Airport was busy, as always. Going through security was sometimes an interesting experience. Her ever-present large hoop earrings, plus the rings and bracelets she wore, occasionally set off the alarms of the metal detector. Thankfully, this time, it all went smoothly. Lucy found her gate, plopped her carry-on bag in the empty chair beside her and closed her eyes. Even though she had made a last-minute decision to book her flight for today and was unable to get a seat in first class, she was looking forward to this much-needed respite from work and life in general. She also needed a break from James, her business associate, who seemed to labor under the delusion their relationship should be more than strictly business. While Lucy craved some down time, she had to admit visiting with her daughter, Victoria, might be challenging, also.

Victoria could be fun if she allowed herself to be. She and her husband, David, had tried the in-vitro method to become pregnant several times, but none was successful. With no children to distract him, David's career had become totally consuming. At least, it seemed that way to Lucy.

Maybe this visit would be different; David was in Europe on a business trip. Victoria worked part-time at a local clothing boutique but could set her own hours. That might allow the two of them an opportunity to enjoy some mother-daughter time.

It seemed like hours before it was time to board. Finally, her flight number was called. Lucy found seat 10B, stowed her carry-on bag in the overhead compartment and squeezed into the aisle seat. Seat 10A was occupied by a handsome man, probably in his 60s, she would guess. He held a book on his lap, which indicated he might read instead of talking the entire flight. Although Lucy considered herself friendly and outgoing, she was looking forward to some time alone with her thoughts.

"Name is Jerry," he said as he held out his hand.

"Louisa." Lucy offered as she shook his hand. He had a firm handshake. Lucy liked that. Grandpa always told her she could tell a lot about someone just by their grip when you shook hands with them.

"Louisa," he repeated thoughtfully. "Not a name you hear too often."

"My mother liked reading Louisa Mae Alcott's books; hence, the name Louisa Mae. When my baby brother came along, he pronounced it Lucy. My business associates know me as Louisa; my close friends and family call me Lucy."

She had explained her unusual name so many times that the story surrounding its origin came out whether anyone asked or not.

"Hmmm, so you live in two worlds…sort of?"

"I guess you could say that. I jokingly refer to it as having a split personality, although that isn't accurate, either. I'm pretty much the same person, regardless of what name someone uses."

Jerry nodded his understanding and smiled. "Going home to Texas?"

"No. Actually, my home is in Chicago. I'm going to visit my daughter who lives in Texas."

As soon as Lucy said those words, they sounded strange to her ears: *My home is in Chicago?* Never. Home would always be in Texas; specifically, Magnolia, Texas, even though the only thing remaining there for her were her memories. Wanting to be alone with her thoughts, Lucy leaned her head back and closed her eyes.

Jerry observed the woman sitting next to him. She was dressed impeccably—business attire, he assumed. She wore lots of jewelry; it was not the cheap, imitation stuff, he noticed, but the real thing. Despite several rings, he also noticed there was no wedding band. If he had to guess her age, he would say she was in her late 50s, although he was a horrible judge of age. She wore her medium-length dark hair pulled into a clip at the nape of her neck. There were a few streaks of gray in it, which obviously didn't bother her as it did most of the women he knew. She struck him as a self-confident, comfortable in her own skin kind of woman.

Lucy dozed for a short time. She dreamed the same dream she had been having for more than a month; it gave her chills, which caused her to wake with a start.

She opened her eyes and noticed Jerry had apparently put his novel in his briefcase and was now reading a Bible.

Great, she thought. *That's just what I need on this trip, a Bible-thumper.*

The attendant rolled a cart down the aisle. Lucy bought a soda; Jerry had a bottle of juice. Jerry chuckled as the attendant continued down the aisle. "I feel old; I remember when they served a nice meal on the flight to Houston. Then they downgraded to crackers, and now you get nothing for free."

Lucy nodded. "Yes, I remember the meals, too. I guess it does date us, doesn't it?"

Finishing her soft drink, she nodded toward his Bible and said, "I know I'm being entirely too nosey but I don't encounter many people on planes reading their Bibles. Are you a preacher or something?"

"Well, I'm not a man of the cloth, so that leaves me as 'something,' doesn't it?"

She smiled and observed he hadn't actually answered her question. Lucy also noticed his tanned face had fine lines around his eyes that crinkled when he smiled. He was muscular, too, at least as far as she could tell while sitting in an airplane seat. And she believed he was close to her age. Maybe this was the cowboy Phoebe thought she should bring home.

She laughed out loud at her thoughts, knowing when she found her cowboy, he definitely would not be reading a Bible. At least, she hoped not.

"Is something wrong?" Jerry asked.

"No. I wasn't laughing at you. It was something I remembered my friend saying when she dropped me off at the airport. I absolutely do not care if you read your Bible."

Jerry smiled at her. "Now it's my turn to be nosey. Do you read your Bible, Louisa?"

"Truthfully, Jerry, I don't have a very good relationship with God any longer. We stopped speaking many years ago. The only Bible I own belonged to my grandmother, and it's packed away somewhere. It's worn and tattered; she read it faithfully."

Lucy's mind drifted to a time right after her parents died in a plane crash. She was only 4 years old but she remembered being cuddled on her Grandma Ivy's lap in the big wooden rocker. Grandma was comforting Lucy, and herself, by reading passages from that Bible. She spoke the words softly until the tears on Lucy's cheeks dried and she fell asleep.

Lucy shook off the memory, jerking her mind back to the present. "It would probably fall apart anyway…*if* I ever felt the need to open it someday."

Jerry smiled at Lucy and again, she was drawn in by his blue eyes and his gentle smile.

"I know you say you stopped talking to God, but he never stopped talking to you. Perhaps you simply need to start listening for his voice again."

"Mmm, maybe," was the best answer she could give him.

* * *

Jerry had often been told his spiritual gift was perceptiveness. Perhaps it was. For one thing, Louisa might be visiting Texas now, but he knew she had lived in Texas at some point in her life. Even though her speech had no hint of an accent to most people, to someone like him who had lived in Texas his entire life, that tiny bit of drawl that never goes away completely was evident. He also knew something was troubling her—perhaps physically or emotionally, but definitely spiritually. He sighed; what could he do? He would add her name to his prayer list and let God take care of the rest. After all, the odds of him ever seeing Louisa again were slim to none.

The rest of the flight was spent in small talk. When they landed in Houston at George Bush Intercontinental Airport, Lucy and Jerry walked off the plane and into the throngs of travelers. They wound their way to the baggage claim area. When she spied her purple bag, she lifted it off the carousel, stood it upright and offered her free hand to Jerry. "It's been nice traveling with you, Jerry." He took her hand, and she was again impressed with his solid, firm handshake.

"Take care of yourself, Louisa. Perhaps we will meet again one day." With that, they parted ways; he was looking for a taxi, and Lucy was headed to the rental-car section.

CHAPTER 2

LUCY HAD RESERVED AND PAID for the rental car online, so she only had to show her ID and grab the keys from the young woman working behind the counter. She retrieved a small box from inside her suitcase and placed it in her purse. She lifted her suitcase into the trunk, then put her smaller carry-on bag and the purse on the passenger's seat.

Whew. The air inside the car was stifling. She rolled the windows down and turned the air control to the maximum setting.

While the interior was cooling down a bit, she called her son to let him know she had arrived safely. The answering machine picked up. "Hello. This is the Newsome home. Speak now or never." Obviously, one of the children recorded that message.

"Hello, Newsome Family. This is Grammy. I made it safely to Houston and am on my way to your Aunt Victoria's house. Bye."

Lucy rolled the windows up, made certain she knew which button or lever controlled the wipers, since every model of car was different, and then turned the radio down.

Okay, Lucy, off you go to the lion's den, also known as Victoria's house. Aloud, she said, "I really hope the Beltway and 290W aren't under construction. But then again, when *aren't* they under construction?"

As she drove, she thought about Jerry. It hadn't entered her mind to give him one of her business cards. If she had, he would at least be able to call her if he wanted. It would be extremely difficult to bring a cowboy home, as Phoebe always told her, if she couldn't even remember to give him her card.

The thought of learning all the new rules to the dating world, if she ever considered entering it again, gave her a headache.

* * *

Forty minutes later, she entered Cypress, an attractive suburb on the northwest side of Houston. The street where Victoria and David lived had large comfortable homes with well-manicured lawns. She eased the car into Vicki's double drive, making sure she wouldn't block the side of the garage where Vicki kept her car. Lucy used her key to unlock the front door. If Vicki wasn't home, she sincerely hoped she had remembered to turn the security system off. When she visited a year ago, Vicki had forgotten. Until then, Lucy hadn't realized Cypress had so many police cars.

Letting herself in, she called, "Vicki. I'm here. It's your wonderful, adorable and loving mother."

Silence. That was okay. She was tired and knew her way to the bedroom she always used when she visited. In fact, she kept clothes in the closet all year long. That eliminated bringing more than one bag when she came for a short stay. Vicki and David had a large house with five bedrooms. It seemed entirely too big to Lucy, especially for two people, but then she didn't have much room to talk. Her historic house in Batavia was also quite large, and there was only *one* of her.

She placed her purse carefully on the nightstand and kicked off her shoes. Rifling through her bag, she pulled out a pair of jeans and a red T-shirt. Lucy quickly undressed, splashed some cool water on her face and put on the clean clothes.

"Ahhh, that's better," she sighed as she flopped across the bed.

When Lucy opened her eyes, the room seemed a bit darker. She hadn't intended to fall asleep. Glancing at the time on her phone, she saw she had a missed call from Phoebe and a message from Victoria. The message told her Vicki wouldn't be home until later that evening, but if she was hungry, she would find ingredients for a sandwich in the refrigerator. Ugh, she didn't want a sandwich. Her stomach was letting her know the bagel she had for breakfast and the soda on the plane were definitely cause for revolt. Lucy rummaged in her closet, found her favorite pair of boots and pulled them on. She checked her hair, made a quick fix to her make-up and grabbed her keys and purse. She would find a place to eat in Tomball, a neighboring town. She had not been there on her last visit. Maybe there was a new eatery.

Lucy drove down the main street but didn't see anything that interested her. It was Sunday, and many businesses closed early. As she neared the outskirts of town, she noticed a building that had obviously been rebuilt and redecorated recently. In large letters over the front swinging doors, the words, Long Branch Cafe, piqued her interest. She chuckled at someone's ingenuity as she read the sign above a hitching rail. "Park your horses or your horsepower here." She promptly parked her horsepower and went inside.

As her gaze swept the interior, she thought she had been transported to the set of *Gunsmoke*. A young girl dressed in western clothes wearing a name tag with "Lacey" written on it, showed her to a table. By this time, Lucy was almost hungry enough to eat the menu instead of waiting for food.

She heard the ringtone that meant an incoming call from Phoebe. "Hey, Phoebe. I made it safely."

"You forgot to call me when you landed."

"I know. I'm sorry. I intended to call when I got to Vicki's house but fell asleep instead. Listen, you would love this place I found. It has been refurbished to look exactly like the Long Branch Saloon. I fully expect to see Miss Kitty come sashaying down the stairway any minute."

"Forget Miss Kitty. Is Marshal Dillon there?"

"Ha. Nope, I don't see him. With my luck, it would probably be Festus, anyway."

Lucy could hear Phoebe cackling. "I will definitely let you know if the Marshal...," Lucy sucked in her breath. "Oh my goodness, Phoebe. You aren't going to believe this, but I believe the Marshal just walked in through the swinging doors."

Phoebe let out a yelp. "What does he look like? Fill me in, Lucy."

She tried to look inconspicuous as she scanned the man from the top of his Stetson cowboy hat to the bottom of his boots.

"I would guess he's around 6'4" tall with broad shoulders, a little gray by his temples, long legs and he obviously has very good taste in hats and boots."

Phoebe chided her. "Only you would be looking at a gorgeous specimen of maleness and be impressed by his hat and boots. You told me your grandpa taught you to ride, rope and shoot. I think the only option here is to rope and hogtie him and bring him home."

Lucy laughed out loud at the picture that flitted through her mind at Phoebe's suggestion.

"Phoebe, have you been drinking?"

"Maybe a glass of wine...or two." She giggled.

"Okay, Phoebe. I'll call you in the morning. Good night."

She and Phoebe had been friends for many years. Collectively, they had been through a divorce, three deaths, financial hardship, starting two businesses, nearly a year in the hospital, raising rebellious teens and much more. The "let's-find-Lucy-a-man joke" had been ongoing for a long time. Lucy couldn't even remember how it started but it would probably never end until she found someone to marry or she died. At this point in her life, the latter was more likely to happen.

Lucy watched him while she drank her iced tea. He seemed to be scanning the room, looking for someone. He had a brief conversation with the hostess, then turned and walked back out onto the sidewalk.

Lacey brought her dinner. When she lingered for a minute, Lucy looked up questioningly.

"He's a great guy," Lacey said as she nodded her head in the direction of the doors.

"Who is a great guy?"

"Cal Frasier, the man who was just in here. I saw you looking at him." Lacey's cheeks reddened as she realized she might have overstepped her bounds.

Lucy smiled. "Yes, I guess I was looking at him. He reminded me of someone I know in Chicago," she lied.

* * *

Cal walked the two blocks to his efficiency apartment. He was glad he had it, as it was easier to stay in town sometimes rather than go back to the ranch, especially if he had business to finish in the morning.

He couldn't help but notice the attractive, dark-haired woman at the Long Branch. She was either new in town or maybe passing through. He noticed the car parked outside had Nebraska plates on it, but it could be a rental. Of course, he didn't know everyone in Tomball, but he knew the regulars at most of the diners, and she definitely was not one of them.

He didn't have time to think about some woman right now. He had a herd of cattle to fatten up. The buyer didn't want to ship them by rail, so they had to be ready to travel on foot for a distance. That was several months away, but things like that took planning. He had promised the cattle to the buyer, and Cal Frasier was a man of his word.

Lucy paid her bill, gathered her keys and purse and walked out into the night. The air was heavy with the scent of flowers and approaching rain. Grandpa always said she had a "nose for coming storms."

Too bad I couldn't foresee some of the approaching storms in my life over the years, she mused.

CHAPTER 3

LUCY WAS RELIEVED TO SEE there were lights on inside the house when she pulled into the drive. Victoria had obviously made it home. When she reached the door, she was greeted with a shout. "Mom, is that you?"

"If it's not me, you would be in trouble, my dear."

Vicki came around the corner, and they embraced in a mutual bear hug.

"It is so good to see you. I'm sorry I wasn't home when you got in earlier…and by the way, where have you been?"

"Let me think, I believe your answer to me when I used to ask you that question, was, 'Oh, nowhere.'"

Vicki laughed. "Yes, but I was a teenager. So, seriously, Mom, where have you been? It's late, and it looks like rain."

"Victoria, Victoria, I'm a big girl, and I can take care of myself."

A frown appeared on Vicki's pretty face. "Yes, I know exactly how you think you can take care of yourself and how you are prepared to do that."

Lucy decided to change the subject. "Can we get out of the front hall and move to the family room so I can take my boots off?"

"Yes, of course. Come on." She followed Vicki to a spacious room decorated in an eclectic blend of modern and traditional with just enough Western influence to make it look homey and comfortable.

Lucy ran her hand over her grandmother's ceramic vase displayed on an end table. It had yellow roses painted on the sides. She gave it to Vicki several years ago while telling her the story of her Great-Grandma Ivy's love of yellow roses. Grandpa always referred to Grandma as his Yellow Rose of Texas. Many varieties of flowers struggle to survive in the harsh weather of the state, but for some reason, Grandma's yellow roses not only survived but thrived. They changed the name of their ranch to the Yellow Rose to remind them, with God's help, they could survive anything. Lucy sighed; it hadn't exactly worked out that way.

Vicki was talking to her, but she had no idea what she'd said.

"What did you say, Honey? My thoughts were off in faraway places."

"I have so many things to share with you, Mom. Would you like a cup of coffee or tea?"

"No. I'm good; I don't usually drink coffee right before bedtime, and I already had one cup with dinner."

They sat next to each other on the sofa. Lucy said to Vicki, "Tell me your news. It must be good news. I can see the happiness on your face."

"Well, you already know the last in-vitro attempt didn't work, like the ones before." A shadow of disappointment and sadness crossed her face, but she continued. "You also know we discussed adopting, but weren't sure we would be comfortable raising someone else's child."

"Yes, you told me about that several months ago. Have you reconsidered it?"

Vicki grabbed her hand and squeezed. "We have not only reconsidered it; we are in the process of being approved for siblings. Two children, Mom! Isn't it wonderful?"

Lucy had to catch her breath. It was good to see the happiness on Vicki's face; it had been a long disheartening time for her and David.

"How long have you known? Why didn't you tell me? Doesn't adopting take a long time? How is this happening so quickly?"

Vicki held up her hand, "One question at a time. I couldn't tell you over the phone; I wanted to see the look on your face so I forced myself to wait until you got here. And yes, it does usually take a long time, but we have an attorney; he's a friend we met at church. He's helping to move things along. There are at least a million forms to fill out, but thankfully, we are on form #500,034 so we are over halfway to being finalized."

Lucy was absorbing all this information as fast as she could, but her thought process hit a little snag at the reference to church. She didn't know her daughter and son-in-law attended a church.

"I can't begin to tell you how happy and excited I am for you and David. Wait," she teased, "that doesn't mean I have to give up my bedroom, does it?"

"No, Mom. We have plenty of bedrooms." She hesitated…then continued, "But you might have to give up your protection when you come to visit after we bring the children home."

Lucy raised an eyebrow at that remark but chose to ignore it for the present.

"More news…David is looking for a different job so he won't have to travel as much; especially not out of the country. Children deserve to have two parents to love and care for them. I know you did a fantastic job raising Paul and me after Daddy died, but I learned from your experiences how hard it is to be a single parent, and David and I agree we both need to be here."

"I agree with you wholeheartedly. It will be wonderful if David finds a position that allows him to be home more. Has he had interviews with a local firm?"

"He has an interview scheduled when he returns to the States next week."

"Your brother has his name in for a new position, also. He's had several headhunters calling him. The downside is he and Lynne and the kids might have to move to another state, depending on the offer he accepts."

"Are Paul and Lynne praying about the decision, Mom? David and I have learned we can't make decisions without God's guidance."

Lucy stared at her daughter for a minute. Her son, Paul, his wife, Lynne and their children were very involved with their church, but who was this person sitting next to her? Vicki had always scoffed at the idea of needing God in her life.

Vicki saw the unspoken questions flitter across Lucy's face. "When we were at the hospital for the last in-vitro procedure, a friend came by to sit with us. She asked if she could pray with us and casually invited us to join her at church when we felt comfortable. We decided to try it; we met friendly, genuinely caring people. We joined a small Bible class, and as they say, the rest is history."

Sensing Lucy's discomfort, Vicki asked, "Now one more thing. You still haven't told me where you were tonight."

"I went back in time about 45 years to Dodge City and the Long Branch Saloon."

Vicki feigned horror. "You found a saloon?"

"Not a real saloon. It was actually a great place called the Long Branch Cafe in Tomball. It looks exactly like the set of *Gunsmoke*, a television series I watched faithfully as a kid. The cast was missing, though, except for Marshal Dillon. He made an appearance."

"I must be tired. I am totally confused."

Lucy explained. "I was talking to Phoebe, describing the inside of the restaurant when a handsome man walked in. I told her Marshal Dillon was there. Marshal Dillon was the star of the television series—a rugged cowboy who always did the right thing. She was instantly sure he was the one I needed to bring home with me."

"Why is Phoebe always looking for a man for you, Mom? You're a beautiful, accomplished, intelligent woman; you own your own business, have more than enough resources to last your entire life, you have James working with you and accompanying you to various functions and as you say, you can take care of yourself. Why does she think you need a man?"

"I don't remember exactly how it started. It is a long-standing joke between us. Maybe she thinks I need someone to grow old with, Vicki, and I can assure you it won't be James. I can also tell you my business and money won't wrap their arms around me or make love to me."

"Mom, TMI...that means too much information."

"I know what TMI stands for, Vicki. Please don't tell me you believe people my age don't make love anymore or have desires for intimate relationships. If you do...guess what? You're wrong."

Vicki shook her head. "I know that in my head, but when that kind of talk is referring to my mother, it doesn't sound right."

Lucy put her arm around Vicki. "Okay, Sweetie. I'll try to steer away from the subject."

"I'm tired, and I'm sure you are too, Mom. How do you feel about going to Spring tomorrow and checking out the craft shops? We can grab lunch at that restaurant on the corner. The one with the open-air seating, remember?"

"That sounds like a perfect idea, Vicki. I like the metal lawn ornaments they have in every shop in Spring, but I don't think I could get one home on the plane. It would be considered a weapon, for sure," she laughed.

They both stood. After a hug, Vicki said, "I almost forgot to tell you. I got an unexpected call from Uncle Leon. He would like to come home for the family Christmas, if that would be okay with you."

The hair rose on the back of Lucy's neck. She had not spoken to her brother, Leon, for 23 years. Not since she found out he squandered his inheritance money and then proceeded to lose the Yellow Rose to some greedy investor. She had never forgiven him, and she sure as heck wasn't spending Christmas with him.

"Christmas is a long way off Vicki, but if your uncle calls again, you can tell him he is not welcome." She walked to her bedroom not waiting for Vicki's answer to what she just said.

Lucy undressed, pulled on a long T-shirt and crawled between the sheets. Just the thought of seeing her brother brought tears to her eyes, not for him but for the fact she would never again call the Yellow Rose Ranch her home. It didn't matter that half of it was supposed to be hers. What mattered was it held every childhood memory she had, and Leon destroyed them all.

As she lay in the dark, she wondered, as she often did, if the ranch house and buildings looked the same as when she lived there, or if the new owner destroyed them all and built something entirely different? She could picture every detail in her mind: the stone and wooden exterior, the circle drive in front of the porch that ran along the entire front of the house. The house had been built for two families; obviously the original owners, her great-grandparents, believed future generations of Hendersons would need the room. There were two large, complete houses on each end of an expanse. Connecting them was a huge room with lots of glass windows and a stone fireplace. It was always referred to as the Great Room, with more bedrooms located above it. The entire family and guests would gather there for birthday parties, cookouts, Fourth of July celebrations and Christmas mornings. There were stables, a bunkhouse, a foreman's house and several other buildings in her memories. There was also a landing strip for the plane her father owned and enjoyed flying.

The tears formed on her lashes, then rolled down her cheeks as she thought of her grandparents and all they had worked for. It was unbelievable how it could disappear in one drunken poker game.

CHAPTER 4

LUCY AWOKE TO THE SMELL of freshly brewed coffee—one of the best smells in the world, in her opinion. As she made her way to the kitchen, she passed the hall mirror and noticed her eyes were still a bit puffy from last night's crying.

"Morning, Mama. Have a cup of coffee."

"Ahhh, I knew there was a reason I choose to stay here instead of a hotel," Lucy teased as she took the cup Vicki held out to her.

"And here I thought it was so you could visit with me," Vicki pouted. "Did you sleep well?"

Lucy inhaled the strong aroma and sat on one of the tall stools around the kitchen island.

"Yes, I did but I have this recurring dream or nightmare, I'm not sure which it is. I haven't told anyone because it seems silly, but I'd like your opinion."

"Sure. Tell me."

"It's the same every time. I'm somewhere nice, maybe a party or reception and everything is lovely. I seem happy, but I have the feeling there is something dark and ominous over my left shoulder. I turn to see it, but it moves out of my peripheral vision. I can never turn fast enough to catch a glimpse."

"That's eerie. How often do you have this dream?"

"It started a few months ago. It happened once a week, possibly, but lately it is nearly every night and even yesterday on the plane."

"I think we need to pray about this, Mom. I believe God is telling you about something or someone who wants to harm you." Lucy dismissed the idea. "I shouldn't have troubled you with this. You have enough to think about with your 500,000 adoption forms. Besides, the dream is probably caused by eating before bedtime," she laughed.

Vicki shrugged her shoulders. "Speaking of adoption forms, our attorney called. He would like to go over some information this morning. Can we postpone our trip to Spring until tomorrow?"

"Of course, Sweetheart. I have some business matters to take care of anyway. My project manager called early this morning with a problem. When you get back, I want to hear the rest of the story about your soon-to-be family. We got sidetracked last night. I didn't ask ages or gender or any of the details."

"I can't wait to tell you everything about them. This appointment shouldn't take long, and then we'll drink iced tea and chat the rest of the day."

"Sounds like a plan. Drive carefully. I'm going to take a shower before I tackle the contractor problems in Illinois."

When Lucy stepped out of the shower, she glanced at her reflection in the full-length mirror. Not too bad for 59 years old, she thought. The personal trainer had definitely helped with some of the sag factor. Her eyes caught the yellow rose tattoo on the top of her left breast. That had been a knee-jerk decision after returning to Magnolia and discovering Leon had lost the ranch. She told herself she needed something to remember her childhood home, and the rose tattoo seemed the logical choice at the time.

She grabbed her jeans, pulled a shirt over her head, brushed her hair and poured a second cup of coffee. She sat down with her phone and laptop.

*   *   *

Victoria was ushered into the attorney's office. "Good morning, Mr. Watkins."

"Please, Vicki, call me Jerry. We see each other every week at church services and pray together, too, at Bible study. There's no need to be formal. Can I get you something to drink?"

"No. I had coffee with my mother before I came. She's visiting for a few weeks and always stays at our house. We have plenty of room."

"Yes, I believe you mentioned that at our earlier meeting. Actually, that's part of the reason for these forms today. As you know, before any adoption can be finalized, every 'T' has to be crossed and every 'I' dotted. The agency wants to know every shred of information about anyone who will live with the children, even for short periods of time."

"I understand. I think I have most of the additional things you needed from me, but I probably should have brought my mother along so she could provide her information."

"Maybe she can do that another day, if it becomes necessary. You can fill in a few of the blanks. Okay, let's get started in the logical place. What is your mother's full name?"

"Louisa Mae Crowder."

Jerry dropped the pen and stared at her. How many women could possibly be named Louisa?

"Tell me, did your mother arrive yesterday on a flight from Chicago?"

"Yes, she did," Vicki answered, looking perplexed.

Jerry smiled. "I knew it. I felt God was telling me I would see her again. I didn't know how or when, but I knew I would."

He realized Vicki had no clue what he was rattling on about. He told her of meeting Louisa on the plane and their conversation.

"Before I fill in any blanks on these forms with detailed information, why don't you, in your own words, tell me about your mother—general things, like her occupation, marital status, health. You know, her life story, only in Cliff Note form." He laughed at his own joke.

He asked himself if he really needed to know the things Vicki was going to tell him or whether he just wanted to know more about Louisa?

"She's pretty complex, Jerry. We could be here all day."

"Let's start with the highlights. If I need more, I will ask her when she comes to the office."

Vicki nodded. "She was born on a ranch outside Magnolia, Texas. It belonged to her grandparents and was named the Yellow Rose Ranch. Her father, Albert, her mother, Selma, and brother, Leon, lived there, also."

"Her parents were killed in a plane crash when she was 4 and Leon was 2. Her grandparents raised her and Leon. She graduated with a bachelor's degree in business. She married my father, they moved to Chicago and after 12 years of marriage, he died of lung cancer. When her grandparents both died within a month, Mom used her inheritance money to start a business that became quite successful. Not too many years ago, she was dazzled by a man who tried to take everything she had. After they divorced, she poured herself into her business, even more than before. She is self-confident and certain she can take care of herself in any situation. Her business is worth millions, I'm sure, but she's also quite generous. It's funny, really, how she can be two people…almost. Not in a negative way, but when she comes to visit in Texas, her business persona is left in Illinois. Here she pulls on her boots and becomes that child again. Occasionally, you might even hear her say, 'y'all.'"

Vicki was pensive for a minute, and then continued, "That reminds me. Will the agency check for registered firearms, Jerry?"

"Yes. That would be a point of consideration. Why? Do you or David own a gun?"

"No. But my mother does."

Jerry raised an eyebrow slightly, but the information didn't surprise him.

"One more thing and this has nothing to do with the adoption process. She turned her back on God years ago. Perhaps we could pray about that at our next Bible study?"

"Yes, of course, Vicki. Well, your mother is definitely an interesting woman. Thank you for sharing those insights. I think I will call and ask her to come in so she can give me her financial information."

When Vicki left his office an hour later, Jerry smiled. He knew when he met Louisa that she was not your average businesswoman. He liked what he knew about her. He was tempted to call her immediately to make the appointment just so he could see the look on her face when she realized her daughter's attorney was her former traveling companion.

* * *

Louisa placed a call to James to ask what was happening with the latest housing acquisitions. Her call went immediately to voicemail, which was not a good sign.

Next she called her project manager. He answered on the first ring. "Anthony. This is Louisa. What's happening with the houses on Gerard Street? Your message said there was a problem."

"Louisa, you aren't going to like this. James came by and told me to pull the crews off Gerard Street. Said you were cutting your losses on that project. I got 'em shut down but thought I should get the word from you directly before we move everything."

* * *

Lucy thought if she were a smoker, she'd be chewing on the end of a cigar by now and maybe gulping down a glass of whiskey, too. Instead she thanked Anthony. "You did the right thing by keeping the crews there. I have not pulled out of Gerard Street. You tell them I will make sure they each get a bonus for their down time, and Anthony, I will make this up to you. Get everyone back to work, okay?"

"You know I will. What do I say to James if he comes back?"

"No worries. I'll handle James."

What on earth was James thinking? He had been the perfect complement to her business when she hired him—hard-working, resourceful. She had done her homework and checked his background thoroughly. He wasn't some young kid recently out of college; he was 45 years old. Lately, he had been edgy, worrying about things that shouldn't have concerned him. But now, stalling a huge project when there was a deadline? When she got back to Illinois, they were going to have a serious talk. Right now, she would have to settle for phone conversation, if he turned his phone on. There might be another way to get a message to him.

Suddenly, Louisa thought of her nightmare. Was James the person who was just out of sight? The thought made her shudder, but she pushed it out of her mind. Surely that wasn't possible.

CHAPTER 5

ON THE DRIVE HOME from her meeting with Jerry, Vicki practiced her "You have to get rid of the gun" speech to Lucy. When she let herself in the side door, Louisa was talking on her phone. Vicki put ice in two glasses and filled them with tea. She pointed to the sun porch, and Lucy nodded her understanding.

In a few minutes, she came to the porch, grabbed her glass and flopped in the lounge chair.

"Is everything okay, Mom?"

"No, I don't think so but I'm praying I managed to get it straightened out until I get home. This was supposed to be a vacation, not a couple of weeks where I continue to work from 1,200 miles away."

Vicki couldn't let the reference to praying go without a comment. "I'm sure it would be a better outcome if you really were praying about it."

"Don't get excited, Victoria. It's just a phrase."

"Tell me what's going on that James can't handle for you."

"Instead of handling the problem, James seems to *be* the problem. He purposely shut down a renovation crew. He knows we're playing beat-the-clock or rather beat-the-oncoming-winter-weather with this project. In a few months, the snow will fly in Chicago, and then not much progress can be made. If my contractors can get the outside work done before winter, they can spend the frigid months doing the inside work. I promised the city these houses would be ready for occupancy in early spring, and they will be, even if I have to hire more finishing crews, which, of course, cuts into the profit margin."

"If James can't handle the job, why keep him? There are surely other capable people needing the work."

"Yes, I'm sure there are. Truthfully, I hate to train a new person. I pay James well for his expertise in dealing with the city and state government forms, but in the last six months something has changed. I pride myself on reading people, but I can't quite put my finger on this."

Vicki raised her eyebrows with a question in her eyes. "He sent a picture of the two of you at some charity event." She flipped through the photos on her phone and held it for Lucy to see.

"That's a beautiful gown you're wearing, by the way. The two of you made quite the handsome couple. Are you sure you aren't romantically interested in him?"

Lucy choked on an ice cube. "Not in the least. But he constantly thinks he's going to persuade me to be interested in him. Besides, he's 14 years younger than me and definitely not my type."

"What is your type, Mom? You thought Derek Crowder was your type, didn't you?"

There was a long pause before Lucy answered. "For a short period of time, I guess I did. Maybe I always knew he wasn't right for me, but he was certainly charming, wasn't he? He knew how to make me feel special. I'm still kicking myself for falling for him. I must have been extremely lonely to marry him. However, they say no experience is wasted if you learn from it."

"What did you learn?" Vicki asked.

Lucy dug deep into past emotions. "I learned when a man is involved, I need to keep my heart walled off, and if a crack appears, I make sure I patch it immediately. I learned never to trust a man who wouldn't leave everything and everyone for me, if it came to that. I learned to never tell anyone what my business is worth financially, and finally, I learned once again that God and I don't see eye-to-eye on this ride called Life."

Lucy stretched her legs. "That's enough about me and my past and present mistakes. Tell me about my prospective new grandchildren."

Vicki's face lit up like a neon sign. "I wish I had pictures, but the agency won't allow us to have any yet. Bethany just turned 2 and Devon will be 4 in November. They look a lot alike, except Bethany's eyes are blue and Devon's are brown. Their mother is incarcerated; she signed the papers giving them up right after Bethany was born. The father is listed as unknown, but the mother swore they had the same father. I don't care, truthfully. David is going to be their father, and that's all that matters. They are living in foster care right now, but Jerry is working overtime to speed things up. Wouldn't it be the best Christmas present in the entire world if they could be our children before Christmas?"

"That would be wonderful, Victoria."

"I pray about it every day, in fact, every minute of every day, almost. Would you pray with me right now, Mom? Please? It would mean so much to me."

"I don't think I remember how to converse with God, Victoria. He probably doesn't want to hear from me, anyway."

Lucy looked into Vicki's eyes and knew she could not deny her child this one thing. They sat next to each other and held hands, just as she and Grandma used to do. Vicki prayed an earnest, heartfelt prayer while Lucy silently asked God to hear her child's prayers even if he hadn't heard her prayers in the past.

"Thank you, Mom. I know that was hard for you. Thank you."

Lucy shrugged. "It's okay, Vic. Let's make some dinner and then maybe tonight we can go to the karaoke club you told me about. It's been an emotionally exhausting day so let's go sing our blues away. Hey, that rhymed; I'm writing my own songs for tonight."

Vicki shook her head and laughed. Her mother had always had the ability to bounce out of a deep conversation and start a new one. They enjoyed the shrimp salad they put together and then watched the evening news while they ate it.

"Okay, my little yodeler, let's go teach 'em how to sing." Lucy pulled her boots on, grabbed her purse and they went out the door.

* * *

When they entered the club, it took a moment to become accustomed to the dim light. Some brave soul was on stage belting out a Beach Boys tune.

"Victoria, over here." Vicki turned to see Jerry and another man from her church, waving them over to a table. They threaded their way through the crowded room and joined them. Jerry stood, held out his hand and said, "Hello, Louisa."

She shook his hand. There was a long silence before Louisa spoke. "It's a rare occasion when I am speechless, but this could be one of those occasions. What are the chances I would have a seat on the plane next to someone who knows Vicki?"

Jerry nodded. "When you consider how many people live in the Houston area and the number of flights that arrive here, I would say the chances are mighty slim, if not downright inconceivable."

Lucy switched her gaze from Jerry to the man sitting next to him. "Now this is even more of a coincidence; my fellow traveler and Marshal Dillon at the same table. I don't know what to say."

She turned to the man at the table with Jerry and thrust her hand out. "Hello, Marshal. My name is Louisa Crowder. My friends call me Lucy."

Taking her hand, he never took his eyes off hers. "I'm Calvin Frasier, and my friends call me Cal. Or occasionally, Marshal Dillon, I guess."

Lucy laughed out loud. "I should probably explain that remark. Last night, I ate at the Long Branch Cafe. I saw you there and while talking to my girlfriend on the phone, I remarked how I thought I had just seen Marshal Dillon from *Gunsmoke* come through the swinging doors. In my head, I have been referring to you by that name ever since."

"I'm flattered you've been thinking of me since yesterday, regardless of what name you gave me."

In the darkened club, it was difficult for Vicki to tell whether her mother was blushing about that or not, but her best guess was that she was not. She was certain Lucy was totally enjoying herself.

The conversation turned to Jerry and Louisa's chance meeting on the plane, the adoption progress, David's adventures in Europe and the other singers.

"Are you going to entertain us with a song tonight, Cal?" Lucy inquired

"No, not tonight. I wouldn't want to scare you off. Maybe the next time."

"Are you asking me out for a next time?"

"Mother," Vicki scolded. "You are so bold. I can't believe you said that."

"It's quite all right," Cal told Vicki. "I'm not offended. I'm a firm believer in the fact there's no wisdom in wasting time. My theory is sometimes it's good to throw convention to the winds and say what you mean. So, Lucy, will you go to dinner with me tomorrow evening?"

"Of course, I will. I've never had dinner with a lawman before. Oh wait, there was that policeman in Chicago," Lucy teased.

They spent several hours chatting and enjoying the entertainment. Some people were surprisingly good, and some were obviously delusional about their singing abilities.

Lucy yawned. "I'm tired. If Vicki's agreeable, I think it's time for us to head for home. It has been an enjoyable evening. Thank you for allowing us to sit at your table."

Cal settled his hat on his head and stood. "I'll walk you two ladies to your car." Turning to his friend, he said, "I'll see you Wednesday, Jerry."

When they reached Vicki's car, he reached for the passenger door. "Let me get the door for you, Lucy. I can pick you up tomorrow evening or if you're more comfortable, we can meet at Diamond Rio."

"I'll meet you there at 7, OK?"

Cal nodded as he closed her door. "See you then."

* * *

"Mother, you haven't stopped smiling since we left the club. Do you think it's wise to go out with a man you've only known for a few hours?"

"You did say he attended your church, right? And he is a friend of Jerry, whom you obviously trust. And we will be eating in a public place. And I am driving my car. And he has beautiful brown eyes."

"You are hopeless. Okay. You are all grown up. I guess you can handle yourself. I hope you know what you're doing."

Lucy was looking out the window. "Oh, Victoria, most of the time, none of us knows what we're doing, but we move forward anyway."

CHAPTER 6

LUCY WAS TAKING BISCUITS out of the oven by the time Vicki came out of her bedroom.

Rubbing her eyes, Vicki expressed surprise. "Wow. I'm impressed, Mom. What's the occasion?"

"Nothing special. Just thought my cooking skills needed a little refreshing. I haven't made biscuits in a long time, and they are the one culinary skill I possess. Except, of course for my killer Texas chili, but I didn't think you wanted that for breakfast."

"Don't be so hard on yourself. You can cook. You certainly fed Paul and me when we were growing up, and I remember when Daddy was still alive you would have friends over for dinner. No one ever complained."

"I can cook a few things really well, and the rest is just, you know, everyday cooking. Nothing spectacular. Your great-grandma tried her best, but I was always too busy being outside with Grandpa. He was teaching me things I thought were much more fun. Like how to stay in the saddle no matter what the horse had in mind, how to handle a gun, how to play poker and last, but not least, how to rope and hog-tie a calf." She paused for a bit. "There have been a few times I wanted to use that last skill when I was in a business meeting."

Vicki smiled, "That would be a sight to behold. You might've had to take your high heels off for that."

Lucy chuckled at the picture in her mind. "Probably."

Vicki suddenly turned and headed back to the bathroom. When she returned, her face was ashen.

"See? Just talking about my cooking is making you sick." Lucy laughed.

"Whew. It must have been something I ate yesterday or a bug I caught from someone at the dress shop. I think I'll pass on breakfast."

"Ok. That leaves more for me." Lucy's mouth was already full of her first flaky, buttery treat.

"We never made it to Spring yesterday. Do you feel good enough to go today?"

"Yes, I think so," Vicki told her.

"Good. On the way home, maybe we can stop at the Clothes Boutique where you work and look at some of their new things?"

"I don't know if you can classify what I do there as work, but it is fun to be there one or two days a week, see the new merchandise, dress the mannequins and make a bit of spending money. Are you looking for something special to wear on your date tonight?"

Lucy grinned. "Maybe. What do you think the Marshal would like? Western, Bohemian, jeans and a blouse?"

"Even though it was rather dark in there last night, I would say from the look on his face when the two of you were talking, he won't care what you wear. He just wants to spend time with you."

"I enjoyed talking to him, too. Interesting man."

"Give it up, Mom. You were enjoying flirting with him."

"Guilty as charged. It's always fun to flirt a little, and sometimes, a woman needs to practice again."

"Hmmm, okay; if you say so."

* * *

Vicki and Lucy enjoyed perusing the craft shops and antique stores in Spring. They found several things that would look good in Vicki's family room and a few for Lucy's house. They ate lunch at the open-air restaurant and then headed to the boutique.

"Help me out, Victoria. How dressy is the Diamond Rio these days? Skirt, jeans, capris?"

"Maybe a little dressier than jeans. How about a denim skirt?"

"Ugh. Never. Definitely not umm...what's the word I'm looking for?"

"Sexy?"

They both laughed. "I guess that could be the word."

"How about this long skirt? It's made from that soft, clingy material. You could dress it up or down with jewelry and the type of shoes you wear."

Lucy tried it on and decided it wasn't so clingy it would look ridiculous on her. She chose a soft mint green sleeveless shell to go with it. She didn't need any accessories as she had enough at Vicki's house. She was sure she could find something to match.

*　*　*

As she dried her hair after her shower, she scolded herself for the butterflies flitting around in her stomach. It was only a dinner date, for heaven's sake. She had certainly gone to dinner with other men, although those were strictly business and usually quite boring. She had a feeling that dinner with Calvin Frasier, aka The Marshal, was going to be anything but boring. He could recite the Gettysburg Address, and she wouldn't be able to take her eyes off his face.

"What do you think, Vic? Sandals, wedges, low boots or...maybe barefoot?" Lucy held three pairs of shoes in her hands for Vicki's consideration.

"I think the wedges would look best. Cal is tall; you can wear something with height and still not come close to being as tall as he is."

Lucy turned back to the bedroom. She wrapped a tooled leather belt around her waist and added a necklace and long feather earrings. She wouldn't wear those in Chicago, but for the time she was in Texas, she would revert to her "cowgirl" image.

As Lucy grabbed her leather purse and prepared to leave, Vicki nodded approvingly. "You look fantastic, Mom. Remember the dating rules, okay?"

"You mean to tell me there are still rules, even when I'm almost 60 years old?"

Vicki chuckled. "Probably more of them now. And don't tell me the line about how rules are made to be broken."

* * *

Louisa drove to the Diamond Rio. She suddenly remembered they had not decided if they would meet in the parking lot or go inside to wait. She didn't have to worry. Like a true gentleman, Cal was sitting on a bench outside the door, waiting for her.

She parked, locked the car and strode to the entrance. As she walked toward this tall, handsome cowboy, she couldn't imagine what they would find to talk about; although she had often been told she could talk to a fence post, and this man was definitely not a fence post.

Cal watched her walk toward him. He felt an entire range of emotions in the few seconds it took for her to reach him. He had work to do; what was he doing taking someone to dinner? What would his kids think of him having a date after so many years? What would he and Lucy talk about all night? What was it about her that fascinated him? She was definitely a striking woman, but it was more than that. He felt a connection of some kind.

He couldn't help but smile at her. "Hi, Lucy. I already gave them my name, so we should have a table in a few minutes. You look beautiful. I'm glad it isn't as dark in here as it was in the karaoke club; maybe we can actually see each other as we talk."

When the hostess called his name, Cal placed his hand behind her back and gently guided her to their assigned table. She felt a small jolt of electricity travel up her spine. If she thought about it, no man had really touched her in a protective way since…she couldn't remember when.

They had no trouble finding topics to talk about. They discussed politics, ranching, places they had been and places they would like to go. By the time their dessert arrived, they were up to more personal subjects.

"You mentioned children somewhere in our conversation. How many do you have and do they live close?" Lucy asked.

"I have three—two daughters and a son. Samantha and her husband, Sean, live in Houston. They have two children. Jackie, her husband, Gary, and their little guy, Gabe, live in Beaumont, and Ben is not married…yet. He has a girlfriend, Candy. Ben lives at the ranch. Do you have grandchildren?"

"I have two now, but if the adoption is successful, I will have four. You already know Vicki and her husband, David. My son, Paul, and his wife, Lynne, have two children: Jarrod is 8 and Annie is 5. They live just a block from me in Batavia, so I get to see them often. Paul is looking to change careers, which means they would most likely have to move. I would miss them so very, very much. Especially Annie. It isn't that I love her more; she has been a Grammy's girl since she was born. We do fun things together when she stays with me. Sometimes we play cards or bake cookies or watch movies. She is currently stuck on *The Little Mermaid.* I believe I have watched it at least 25 times. She's missing me. She's called me every day I've been here."

They continued talking long after the server cleared the table. When it appeared the restaurant was going to close for the night, Cal pushed his chair back and helped her with hers. "I'll follow you home to make sure you get there safely. It's late, and you never know what might happen to your car on the way."

Lucy assured him it wasn't necessary, but he insisted.

She could get used to having some man watch out for her. She sighed; some days being self-sufficient was extremely tiring.

As they walked across the parking lot, Cal stopped and turned to her. "I have an idea. If you're free tomorrow, would you like to go riding? Ben is bringing a few horses into Magnolia for a buyer. I could have him bring two extra ones, and we can ride for the day. I'll even have him bring a picnic lunch. What do you think, Lucy?"

"I think I'm happy Ben is bringing the lunch and you aren't depending on me." She laughed at her own joke. "I think riding tomorrow sounds like heaven. It has been a while, but I'm sure I can still manage to stay in the saddle."

Cal followed her home, got out when they arrived at Vicki's house and walked her to the door. When she turned around, she was dangerously close to him. The scent of his cologne and his closeness gave her goosebumps.

"I enjoyed the evening, Lucy, and I'm looking forward to tomorrow. Do you know how long you will be staying in Texas?"

"We-l-l-l, Marshal, that depends on two things," she drawled.

"What are those two things?" Cal asked, not sure he wanted to know.

"The first one hinges on whether or not I can get some business situations settled from here."

"And the second?"

"The second depends on whether or not you kiss me good night."

He traced a line down the side of her face with his fingertip as she looked up at him expectantly, with her lips slightly parted.

Cal leaned over and kissed her softly. When she put her arms around his neck and moved in closer, he put his hand on the back of her head, pulled her toward him and kissed her longer and more passionately.

When they parted, she told him, "I hope Vicki isn't peeking out the window. I always told my kids they should never kiss on a first date."

She opened the door and went inside, humming the lyrics from the *Little Mermaid* movie about wanting to "kiss the girl."

CHAPTER 7

LUCY WAS EXCITED about a day of riding and enjoying Cal's company. She called Phoebe while she drank her morning coffee to tell her about last night's date. Although Phoebe took delight in teasing her about bringing a cowboy home, it was meant as an ongoing joke. She didn't expect Lucy to actually find someone she might care about. There was a long pause on the other end of the line before Phoebe recovered enough to say something. She didn't sound nearly as excited about the planned day of riding as Lucy thought she would.

"Be careful, my friend. Remember you are coming home in another week, and this will all seem like a dream. Right?"

"I suppose you're right, Phoebe. But I'm still going to enjoy this day. Gotta' go, the Marshal is knocking on the front door. I'll call later, okay? Bye."

Lucy glanced briefly at her reflection in the hall mirror on her way to the door. She had chosen a lightweight western shirt and skinny-legged jeans so they would fit inside her boots.

As she opened the door, she said, "Ten o'clock; on the dot. I like punctuality in a man."

"One of my many admirable traits, Miss Lucy."

Cal removed his Stetson and stepped inside while Lucy gathered a light jacket, her hat and a small leather bag to store her phone and a few other essentials. Vicki had left for the clothing shop an hour ago, so Lucy locked the door behind her. Cal led the way to his car and opened the door for her.

"So, exactly where are we riding today?"

"I thought we would start on the outskirts of Magnolia, circle around to the far side of the hill country and have our picnic by the creek that runs through that flat area. There are some trees there, and the horses can rest and drink."

"If I'm remembering correctly, that's close to where the Yellow Rose property line used to be," she commented rather wistfully, more to herself than to Cal.

She glanced at Cal and thought she saw a muscle in his jaw twitch and a surprised look cross his face for a fraction of a second. Maybe she had imagined it; he seemed perfectly okay now.

When they stopped outside Magnolia, Cal's son, Ben, was already there with the horses.

"Nice setup," Lucy commented as she checked out the dark green truck and matching horse trailer. The truck had a large B in the center of a gold star, painted on the cab doors. The trailer had the same emblem on each side.

"Ben, I want you to meet Louisa Crowder."

Ben looked like his father, with lighter hair and blue eyes. She shook hands with him. "It's nice to meet you, Ben. Please call me Lucy."

Ben shook her hand, and then turned to Cal. "I'll stay here until the buyer comes. You can bring the horses back to Gravely's when you're done riding. He said it would be okay to put them in his stable until I come back later. I've got 'em saddled and ready to go. Oh, and your lunch is in the truck in a small cooler."

"Thanks, Ben. As always, you are efficient."

Ben laughed. He slapped his dad on the back while he winked at Lucy. "I learned from the best."

Cal tied the small soft-sided cooler to the back of his saddle. He handed the reins of a black gelding to Lucy. She swung up onto its back as easily as a teenager. He mounted the taller horse, and they walked them out of the pasture where they had been grazing.

"It's been a long time since I've ridden, but it's like the cliché about riding a bicycle—you never forget. I enjoy everything about it: the smell of leather, the creak of the saddle, the sound of the horses' hooves hitting the ground. Believe it or not, I even like the smell of horse manure," Lucy stated.

Cal chuckled. "That's because when you're riding, you can move away from that smell quickly."

The morning was beautiful. The weather was cooler than it had been; there was enough of a breeze to keep any mosquitoes at bay and keep the flies off the horses.

"I hope you don't mind me asking, Lucy, but why do you stay in Chicago? You seem very much at home here in Texas."

"I ask myself that same question occasionally, Cal. I don't know if I have the answer. I like what I do. I enjoy the sights and sounds and activities available in Chicago. I adore my house; I saved it from a wrecking ball and don't want to abandon it now. I must admit, though, the commute gets harder every winter and with each passing year. If Paul and his family move, I won't have anything but my best friend, Phoebe, and my business to keep me there."

They rode in silence for a while, enjoying each other's company.

Cal asked, as if it was an afterthought, "What exactly is your business? Could you do the same thing here?"

"I might be able to, but frankly, I don't have the energy to start over in a new place. I deal with a lot of government agencies and officials. I would have to learn all the legal scenarios again, because each state is different. I would have to prove my abilities and, let's say, *toughness* again. Right now, Louisa Crowder commands respect, no matter how corrupt the official is. She has a reputation for being honest, can't be bribed or bought or slept with, and is as much of a hard-ass as any man they deal with. She won't take no for an answer, and there isn't anything they can slip past her. Believe me, they've tried. If that sounds egotistical, and I know it does, please forgive me; it is a persona I had to build to be able to succeed in the world where I work."

Cal smiled to himself. He could picture Louisa standing up to officials in suits *and* men in hard hats. He also had the picture of the slightly vulnerable woman he kissed last night. Frankly, he liked both images.

The sunshine, the fresh air, the comfortable feeling of being on a horse and enjoying the quietude combined for a therapeutic morning for Lucy. She glanced sideways at the tall man riding the big bay horse next to her. She felt like she had known him her entire life instead of only three days.

"You look pretty comfortable. I guess you were correct when you said you remembered how to ride," Cal told her.

"My father was an only child. When he died, my brother was only 2, so Grandpa made a conscious effort to teach me everything he had previously taught my dad. He gave me my own horse, a black-and-white Paint I named Harmony, when I was quite young. I loved that horse. I rode her without a saddle most of the time, much to my grandmother's dismay. Grandpa would calm her fears by saying, 'Ivy, that girl can ride like the wind. She won't ever fall off.'"

Cal listened as she reminisced. It seemed as if Lucy was speaking to herself and had forgotten he was there.

"He took me along when he and the ranch hands rounded up calves for branding. I learned to rope, and eventually I could wrestle those calves to the ground and tie them. He placed a Smith and Wesson in my hands when I was 8 years old. He made sure I knew all the safety rules. I remember him saying, 'A gun is not a toy, Lucy Mae. Don't ever aim it at anything or anyone unless you plan on using it.' He would set cans on fence posts and have me practice until I never missed. His instructions are ingrained in my brain: Be sure of your target and beyond. Check your stance. Make sure of your grip. Exhale. Follow through. Take your shot."

"He also taught me to play poker. There was a time when I wondered why he thought I needed to know all those things, but I believe Grandpa was much smarter than I realized. He knew I might not need to know how to rope calves or play poker in the real world, but he also knew I would need those life skills in any line of work I pursued. Perseverance, practice, hard work and a self-confident attitude have been very useful. And, I can't tell you how many times I've used the emotionless poker face when negotiating a deal."

Lucy laughed, suddenly realizing she had been talking non-stop for 10 minutes.

"I'm so sorry. You didn't ask for an entire litany of my childhood, did you?"

Cal smiled at her. "You had an interesting life, and obviously your grandfather loved you very much. He called you Lucy Mae?"

"Yes, he and Grandma were the only ones ever allowed to call me Lucy Mae. I guess you could say someone would have to know me really well before I would allow them to call me that. Lucy is good...just plain Lucy."

"Tell me about your childhood, Cal. Have you lived in Texas all your life?"

"No, not exactly. I was born here, but my mother hated everything about Texas—the heat, the cattle, the fire ants and most of all, the loneliness. She was raised in New York City and couldn't adapt to the change. When I was 5, she filed for divorce and took me and my sister back east with her. We lived with my grandparents for a while until she remarried. I would come to the ranch for a few weeks every summer. After I graduated from college, my dad called and offered to make me a partner in the ranch. He wasn't in the best of health and was concerned the land wouldn't remain in the family after he died. I jumped at the chance; I had always loved the ranch and was anxious to use the skills I'd learned to improve the breeding programs. When he died, he willed it to my sister and me. She wasn't interested, so I bought her out. Kathy and I were married and had the three children there. She was diagnosed with breast cancer 12 years ago. It was in remission for a while, but when it returned with a vengeance, she lost the battle. That was 10 years ago. It's been me and the livestock ever since."

"I'm sorry about your wife. Losing someone we love is the most difficult experience. I don't know if I ever truly forgave John for dying and leaving me with two young children."

They rode in silence for a while, each lost in thought. When they found a shady spot, Cal tethered the horses by the creek and Lucy spread the blanket Ben had so thoughtfully packed.

"There isn't much room in that cooler," Cal said. "It will be interesting to see how inventive the cook at the ranch was this morning."

He pulled out gourmet crackers, chunks of cheese and hard salami, grapes, and for dessert, chocolate chip cookies. The pièce de resistance was a small bottle of white wine and two plastic collapsible cups.

They laughed at drinking wine out of cups that could *fold up* at any moment. They toasted their day's adventure.

After they packed the leftovers into the cooler, Lucy sat on the blanket and commented, "I could stay right here forever."

Cal sat behind her and rubbed her shoulders. "Tired?" he asked.

"As inviting as a nap sounds, I don't want to squander a minute of this day. Someone once told me 'You can sleep when you're dead.'"

Cal pulled her hair to the side and caressed the nape of her neck. She turned her face to him and smiled, but suddenly stood and offered her hand to pull him to his feet. "Come on, Marshal. We need to get going or you'll have to arrest me for indecent behavior."

They untied the horses, mounted and rode along a path worn in the prairie grass. Lucy suddenly pulled up and looked around.

"This is the far corner of what used to be my grandparents' ranch. If I'm not mistaken, their graves are right over that next rise, tucked under a tree."

"Do you want to see if we can find it?" Cal asked rather reluctantly.

Lucy hesitated. "I haven't been this close to the property since the day they were buried there. I don't know if I want to go or not."

She debated for a few minutes. "I guess I would like to see if the stones are still there or if the unscrupulous owner destroyed them like he probably did with everything else about the Yellow Rose."

She led the way toward a small plot of ground. The weathered stones were barely visible. Years of neglect and weeds growing inside the perimeter of the rusted iron fence nearly obscured the headstones. Lucy sat ramrod straight and made no effort to dismount or ride closer. Cal rode a little closer, then dismounted and walked to the gate hanging on one hinge. He pushed his way inside. Maybe if he could clear a bit of brush out of the way, Lucy would come closer and at least look at the gravestones of the people who seemed to have been a big part of her life.

He squatted down, removed his gloves and started clearing the debris. That's when he heard it—the telltale rattling sound of a diamondback before it strikes. He obviously disturbed it when he moved the leaves where it was napping.

Before Cal could think, he heard another sound—the ear-splitting, thunderous bark of a revolver. The snake's body was badly torn in two places. The head and a portion of its body hung awkwardly as it writhed in agony. His shirt had flecks of snake flesh, bits of dirt and a few fragments of the bullet's copper jacket clinging to it. When he turned, Lucy was casually slipping the gun back into her boot.

Neither of them said a word. He helped her dismount and heard her say softly, "That was for you, Grandpa. Sorry I didn't have time to do all the things you taught me before I squeezed the trigger."

"I'm sure your grandfather is proud of you, Lucy, and if it were possible, I would definitely like to thank him for teaching you to shoot."

Cal could not believe how foolish he had been to take his leather gloves off. He knew better than that. What was he thinking? His thoughts came full circle, and he knew exactly what he was thinking.

Lucy clung to him for a long time. They seemed to be frozen in place. After what seemed like an eternity, she loosened her grip on his shirt.

"You saved my life, you know," Cal told her.

She smiled. "Maybe one day, you can return the favor and save mine."

"Would you like to take the rattler home? I know someone who would make a nice headband out of the skin."

"No. I think I'll pass. Let's let him rest in peace."

They turned the horses around and rode back the way they had come.

CHAPTER 8

LUCY'S ALARM WOKE HER at 8:30. She didn't remember setting the alarm last night before falling asleep. All she remembered was the wonderful day of riding yesterday and the sweet taste of Cal's kisses when he brought her home. Her phone chirped, and she suddenly remembered why the alarm was beeping. She was supposed to be wide awake and waiting for Phoebe's phone call.

"Hello Phoebes. What's up, friend?" She tried sounding awake while she made her way to the kitchen and the coffee pot.

"So, how was your riding date? I called but you weren't home yet. Did you ride around the entire perimeter of the state of Texas?"

"Yes, as a matter of fact, we did, Phoebe. We rode until the horses fell over and died, and then we made mad, passionate love under the stars. How's that for a report on my day?"

There was silence on the other end of the call. Finally, Phoebe spoke. "You don't need to be so defensive."

"And you don't need to hit me with the Spanish Inquisition so early in the morning. What's wrong? You can't possibly dislike Cal since you don't know one single thing about him."

"I dislike the fact he seems to be sweeping you off your feet just like Derek Crowder did, and we both know how that ended, right?"

Phoebe was the only person who knew the entire story about Derek Crowder.

"Cal is nothing like Derek. He's polite, responsible, church-going, a widower, and he has enough of his own money, if that's what you're worried about."

"A church-going man," Phoebe said sarcastically. "How nice. Since when was attending church one of your requirements in a man?"

"Can we talk about something else, Phoebe? I promise I'll call you if I decide to run away to Vegas with Cal and get married. You can meet us there and be my maid of honor."

"Oh, Lucy. You scare me. Every time you fall for someone, they aren't who they say they are and you end up getting hurt, but as you constantly remind me...you can take care of yourself."

"Yes I can. How's the weather in Chicago? Any predictions about when the winter snows might begin?"

"They're predicting a bad winter so we should enjoy the fall weather first, I guess. You're still returning next weekend?"

"I think so. I'm planning on next Saturday. At least that's when my flight is scheduled."

"Okay. I'll talk to you before then. Take care. Love you."

"I love you, too, Phoebe."

Lucy poured a second cup of coffee, sat down and closed her eyes. She hadn't seen Vicki yet but had heard her retching in the bathroom. The flu bug must still be affecting her, poor baby.

Vicki walked into the kitchen, looking a little green.

"Oh, Sweetheart, why don't you go back to bed and get some rest. Can I make you a cup of tea?"

"No, I'll pass. I haven't been sick in years. I remember why I don't want to be. How are you this morning and how was your day?"

"My day was wonderful, but now I think I have a headache from playing *20 Questions* with Phoebe."

"She's trying to protect you from yourself, Mom. We all are. By the way, you haven't said anything about the nightmare for a couple of mornings. Has it stopped?"

"It did stop for two nights, but it was back last night. I really wish I knew what or who was hanging over my shoulder."

"Would you like to pray about it? It might give you some peace and perhaps the dream will even stop."

"Vic, I..."

"Come on, Mom. It can't hurt, right?"

"Right."

They prayed the dream would disappear or God would grant Lucy peace and guidance to deal with whatever it signified.

* * *

"I'm going to get dressed and do a small load of laundry. What are your plans for the day?" Lucy asked.

"I have some phone calls to make. Jerry would like both of us to meet with him later, if we can. He needs a few things like your social security number and some income figures. He would probably like you to come by yourself. I think he likes you, Mom."

Lucy raised an eyebrow but agreed to go. *And I'll probably get a lecture about my little ol' Smith and Wesson, too,* she thought as she loaded laundry into the washer.

* * *

Cal dialed Jerry's number. "Jerry? I'm sorry I forgot about the planning meeting at church last night. That was unforgivable of me. I got distracted, and it slipped my mind."

He felt relieved that Jerry accepted his apology without further explanation. It wasn't a lie. He had definitely been distracted. Lucy had a way of making him forget everything except her. What had happened to him? He was a disciplined person, devoted to the business of horses and cattle. He had a ranch to run. He hadn't even dated anyone since Kathy died, much less felt the way he was feeling about Lucy.

* * *

Cal's son, Ben, dialed his sisters' numbers for a three-way call. He was excited; he hoped they would be, too.

"Sam, Jackie, hi. You will never believe this."

"Tell us, Ben. Are you and Candy getting married?"

"Yeah, it's about time. You've been dating forever."

"No, it's not me. It's Dad."

"Dad is getting married?" the sisters said in unison.

"Well, I didn't say he was getting married, but he has a girlfriend."

"How do you know that?"

"I saddled two horses yesterday so they could go riding all day. They even took a picnic. I haven't seen Dad look that happy in a long time."

"You have got to be kidding, Ben. What about Mom?"

"Jackie, come on. What about Mom? She died 10 years ago. Don't you think Dad deserves some happiness, or do you want him to turn into a bitter, lonely old man?"

Samantha responded, "Maybe he could join some church groups or something if he wants companionship."

Ben looked at his girlfriend, Candy, who was listening to this exchange, and rolled his eyes.

"Listen, ladies, I hate to tell you this, but our father is not so old that all he needs is companionship or to play bingo on Thursday nights at the church. He needs somebody to love who will love him back and make him feel like a man. And I gotta' tell ya' if anybody could do that, it might be Lucy."

"Who exactly is Lucy? Do you know her last name?"

"Her full name is Louisa Crowder. Why do you care?"

"Where did she come from and how did he meet her? I would bet anything she is some struggling woman who needs Dad's money."

"I don't know much about women's clothes, but I can tell you the boots she was wearing didn't come from a second-hand store. I think she looks like a lady, and I would guess she has her own money to be able to afford them."

"You're right, Little Brother, you *don't* know anything. We need to meet her. Can we plan a family get-together or something so we can check her out?"

Jackie added, "We're free next weekend on Saturday. How about you, Samantha?"

"Yes. Saturday works for us. Ben and Candy, can we all meet at the ranch? We'll make it a potluck and see if she even knows how to cook."

"Ben, you are in charge of getting Dad and his lady friend there, okay? You've got over a week to convince them to be there."

"Sure. Do you want me to warn him you two are going to grill Lucy instead of steaks?"

"Of course not, silly. We're just protecting Daddy, that's all."

"What makes you think a man 62 years old needs protection?"

"Let us know what time is good, okay?"

Ben looked at Candy after he hung up. "I should never have called them. I thought they would be happy for Dad. Now I feel bad. I hope Lucy is a strong woman. She has two barracudas coming after her."

* * *

"David?" Vicki said.

"Hi, Sweetheart. This must be important if you're calling me in the middle of the day."

"It is important. First, I miss you terribly and can't wait until you come home. I have an ulterior motive, though. Do you remember the name of the person you know who works in the Montgomery County Land and Records Office?"

"Sure. It's Darcy Hollister, but why do you need to talk to her? Are you buying us another house?" he joked.

"No. I want to check on a few things. Also, how do I go about finding a person's net worth?"

"I don't think you can. That's private information, Victoria. Who exactly are you investigating and why?"

"It's Calvin Frasier. And yes, I know he goes to our church, but not everyone who attends a church is doing the right thing, you know. I'm worried about Mom and her relationship with him. I know this sounds unbelievable, but I think she is falling in love with him, and she's known him for less than a week."

"Calm down, Vicki. Are you forgetting who Louisa is and what she does for a living? I think she's perfectly capable of handling herself in any circumstance. Besides, I think it would be great if your mother found someone. Let it go. Please?"

"Okay, I will, I guess. Love you. See you soon."

"Men," Vicki muttered after she hung up. "What do they know?" She promptly found the Land Office number and wrote it down for later when Lucy wasn't home.

* * *

Cal dialed a number he hadn't used in a very long time. He reached an answering machine, but left a message. "Leon? Leon Henderson? This is Cal Frasier. I know you know who I am. Please return my call. We need to talk. It's urgent. You have my number."

CHAPTER 9

LUCY HEARD THE BLOOP, bloop, bloop sound from her computer, signifying an incoming Skype call.

When she answered, the sweet face of her 5-year-old granddaughter appeared in front of her.

"Annie. Good morning, Sweetheart. It is so nice to see you."

"Hi, Grammy. I miss you. When are you coming home? Nobody here wants to watch *The Little Mermaid* with me."

Lucy smiled to herself. *Imagine that,* she thought.

"I'll be home in a week, Annie. Do you think you can wait that long? Maybe you can come with Daddy to pick me up at the airport. Would you like that?"

"Yes, oh yes. You ask him, okay, Grammy? He might tell me no. Do you know what I can do? Guess, Grammy, guess."

"Umm, let's see...you can read the newspaper? You can tie your shoes? I know...you can drive a car."

"No-o," Annie giggled. "I can ride my bike without the training wheels. Really, I can. Daddy took them off last Sunday. He had to run down the sidewalk with me a couple of times, but now I can do it all by myself and I don't even fall over. Mommy says I'm like a Weeble. I wobble, but I don't fall over."

Lucy wondered if Annie knew what a Weeble was. They were the toys her children had played with, but she wasn't sure they were still around. She made a mental note when Vic and David got their little ones, she would have to reacquaint herself with the toy department at Toys "R" Us.

"Oh, Annie, I'm so proud of you. I remember when your daddy first rode without his training wheels. He felt so grown up. I bet you do, too."

"Yes, I do. I can't wait to show you, so hurry up and come home. Ok Grammy?"

"Ok, Sweet Girl. Remember to always wear your helmet when you ride."

"I do. We all wear our helmets. Mommy and Daddy say we have to."

"That's a good thing, Annie. I will see you soon. I love you. Tell your brother, Jarrod, I love him, too."

"I will. Gotta' go. Bye."

As fast as her cherubic face had appeared on the screen, it was gone. Not all modern technology was good, but Skype was something Lucy enjoyed.

She folded her clean clothes and took a shower. Her appointment with Jerry was in a few hours, and she wanted to make a salad before she went. She had learned not to enter a possible nerve-wracking meeting on an empty stomach.

Her phone rang before she could make it to the kitchen. Without looking at the number, she answered.

"Lucy?"

Every fiber of her being stiffened, but she said nothing.

"Lucy? This is Leon."

"I know who you *are*, Leon."

"Please hear me out, Lucy. I have some things I need to tell you...about the Yellow Rose."

"Unless you can tell me the events of 23 years ago are a bad dream, I have nothing to talk to you about."

"I'm different now. I've been clean and sober and free of gambling, too, for 10 years. I have a good job and a lady I love, and I really need to clear up some...

Lucy pushed the end call button on her phone and threw it across the room where it landed on the couch.

*   *   *

She arrived at Jerry's law office a few minutes early. She flipped through the pages of a magazine while she waited. The call from Leon had rattled her. Why should she care if he was clean and sober? Too bad he wasn't when he needed to be.

Jerry's secretary asked if Lucy would like something to drink while she waited.

Lucy glanced down at the clean white blouse she was wearing this morning and declined the offer, as she was notorious for dripping at least one drop of liquid down the front of her shirt when she drank in the car or before an important meeting of some kind.

She glanced around the small but impressively decorated waiting room. She would guess Jerry had numerous wealthy and influential clients.

As Lucy was wondering if Cal was one of them or if they were church friends only, Jerry opened the door to his office and extended his hand.

"Hello, Louisa. It's nice to see you again. Thank you for coming. Is Victoria with you?"

Lucy shook his hand and was again impressed with his grip, just as she was the first time on the plane. She couldn't explain it, but Jerry's casual dress in the office, reading a Bible on the plane, talking to her about listening to God—none of those characteristics fit the stereotypical image of any lawyer she had been acquainted with in the past. She sensed there was more to this quiet man than most people realized.

"Vicki said she had some business at the court house and thought you really only needed information from me. I hope that is correct?"

"Yes. You are the 'missing piece' here," he laughed.

"Okay, let's get started. I will tell all, as they say in the movies."

"Before we begin, can I offer you a cup of coffee, a soda perhaps or water?"

Lucy was about to decline again, but changed her mind.

"Yes, thank you." Glancing down at her blouse, she continued, "I don't think I can cause too much damage if I drink water. However, depending on the questions you ask, I might need something stronger," she quipped.

"That could be arranged," was Jerry's answer.

"Let's begin with your physical address in Illinois."

"I live in Batavia, a beautiful place northwest of Chicago."

Lucy gave him her house number and name of her street, her Social Security number and details about her car, her office address and the name of her bank.

Jerry cleared his throat. "Now, I'm sorry to say, I need the information about your personal and business assets. Account numbers, cash-flow charts and, of course, any debts you may have."

"I know it seems a bit much since you don't actually 'live' with David and Victoria and only spend a few weeks at their home a couple of times a year. But, the agency is adamant about knowing everything about anyone who has close contact with the children, even if it isn't on a daily basis. And since we are asking them to accelerate this case as fast as possible, I have to be careful *and* compliant."

"I understand completely. I especially understand any agency under a government umbrella. I will give you anything you need, but I don't keep those figures with me. Can I have my accountant send the information by private currier? I feel safer with that than having it faxed; too many people have access to faxes, I have found."

Jerry nodded his head in agreement and understanding.

"That's perfect. Now let's tackle the subject of the gun you own and carry with you, Louisa."

"Vicki has already told me I have to choose between staying at her house and owning a gun," she laughed.

Then in a serious voice, she told Jerry, "I would never, ever do anything to jeopardize this adoption. David and Vicki have been through so much heartache and disappointment with the unsuccessful in-vitro procedures. Then they had to reach a place in their thinking where adoption was even an option for them, and obviously their involvement in your church helped with that. Now that they are this close to being loving parents to two children, I will do anything to help make that happen."

"Including giving up the firearm I understand was a gift from your grandfather and means a great deal to you?"

There was only a slight hesitation before Lucy spoke. "Yes, when the time comes, I will."

Jerry leaned back in his chair and placed his hands behind his head while gazing at Lucy.

"Louisa, you strike me as an amazing woman. First, I'd like to ask you to join me for lunch on Saturday. Secondly, I'd like to ask you a personal question, if I may."

The lunch invitation took Lucy by surprise, but she agreed to meet him at a small Italian restaurant in Cypress.

She continued the conversation where it had stopped before he asked her. "Yes you may ask anything. But first, let me ask you why you continue to call me Louisa when nearly everyone calls me Lucy?"

"You look like a Louisa to me, and it was how you introduced yourself when we first met, remember?"

"Yes, I do. You can call me either; I have no preference. Now, about that personal question."

"Vicki told me a bit about your marital history, and as I understand it, the second marriage was quite short-lived and didn't end well. Why have you kept the name Crowder? It seems to me it would only bring bad memories. It is really a simple and painless matter to revert to your first husband's name. Then it would also be the same as your son's last name and Victoria's maiden name. I'm certain your attorney in Illinois would do that for you in a heartbeat."

Lucy looked at Jerry for a long time. Finally she said, "You know, Jerry, I rarely drink alcohol of any kind and never in the middle of the day, but if you were serious about that drink, this might be the time for a shot of something stronger than water."

CHAPTER 10

FRIDAY ARRIVED WET and dreary. Cal called Lucy, asking if she would like to make a second visit to the karaoke club that evening. She considered the fact Victoria was going out with a group of church friends, so it was the perfect invitation.

"Vicki, I think I will try singing tonight at karaoke. What song do you think is a good one? You know, I'm not exactly a songbird, so I need one with a melody that isn't too difficult."

"I didn't know you were going back there."

"Cal called and invited me. You weren't going to be home, and besides, I like his company."

Vicki frowned. "How about John Denver's song, *Leaving on a Jet Plane*? After all, next week, you will be leaving and this affair will be forgotten, right?"

"Wow. Where did that attitude come from? Get out of bed on the wrong side? I wouldn't exactly call a few dates an affair. And, no I hope it won't be forgotten. I like him, a lot, and he likes me, I think."

"Did you really give him a choice, Mom? You weren't exactly subtle that first night you met him. If I remember correctly, you asked him out on that first date. You've been acting like a lovesick teenager. Why don't you chalk it up to a fun couple of weeks, like summer camp? You know, every girl falls in love during summer camp, and two weeks after she's home, she can't remember the boy's name. Even if she remembers his name, it's guaranteed, he won't remember hers."

"You know, being the parent of an adult child really stinks. I'd like to send you to your room right now, but that doesn't work so well when the 'child' is 32 years old."

"Or when the parent is living in the child's house," Vicki countered.

* * *

Lucy changed her mind about having a cup of coffee at Vicki's house. She grabbed her purse and keys instead. She drove to the closest coffee house and drank her morning coffee, alone with her thoughts. Was Vicki right? Was everything she said true? Lucy had asked Cal on their first date, and she had asked him to kiss her that very first night. But it was his idea to go riding, wasn't it? Maybe he would be relieved when she was gone. Why hadn't he shown her his ranch when they went riding? It surely couldn't have been too far from where the Yellow Rose had been. And, except for his son Ben, she hadn't heard much about his family.

Lucy drained her cup and went back to her car. This was too much for her brain this morning. First, it was yesterday's meeting with Jerry, then the phone call from Leon, now Vicki's attitude this morning. She had come to Texas for a little R&R not for an entire wagonload of troubles. She would go with Cal tonight and have a good time, have lunch with Jerry tomorrow, attend church with Vicki on Sunday morning, as she promised, and then concentrate on the problems awaiting her when she returned to Illinois.

* * *

They met at the karaoke club even though Cal offered to pick her up. She thought there would be less 'closeness' that way.

Lucy was sorely tempted to tell him what Vicki had said when the emcee called her name to come to the stage. She climbed on a stool, hooked the heels of her boots over a rung and adjusted the height of the microphone.

"Since I am only visiting the great state of Texas and leaving next week, I thought this would be an appropriate song for tonight," she told the audience.

She tried not to look at Cal as she sang the verses and then the chorus, ending with the words, 'I hate to go.'

She received a round of applause as she walked back to their table. Cal was studying her as she came toward him. What would he do when she left? Go back to being lonely, with horses and cattle for company? Should he follow her to Illinois? Ask her to stay here? None of the options seemed feasible. Could he really be that attached to a woman he had only known for a few days?

They stayed a while longer and then made their way to the parking lot.

"Is something troubling you this evening, Lucy? You seem distracted and distant."

"Vicki and I had a mother-daughter difference of opinion this morning. Oh, I almost forgot to tell you—Leon called me again. Of course, he was babbling about being clean and sober and needing to tell me something about the Yellow Rose."

"Did you listen to what he had to say?"

"No. I hung up on him. He has nothing to say I would want to hear."

Cal shook his head a bit. "You know, Lucy, I really think it would be a wise idea to hear him out. Someday, you are going to have to make peace with Leon; if not for him, then for you. You need some peace about the whole situation."

"Really? What gives you the right to lecture me about Leon? This is really none of your business, Cal. Please stay out of it." She turned her back, got in her car and drove out of the parking lot.

Cal pushed his hat back and said under his breath, "Oh Lucy, if you only knew how much it is my business."

* * *

When she came in the front door, Vicki was already home.

"You're home early, Mom. How did the singing go?"

"As good as can be expected, I guess. I'm not exactly John Denver."

Vicki wondered what happened during the evening to make Lucy so irritable. Maybe her mother listened to her advice and told Cal Frasier she didn't want to see him anymore. Ha. Fat chance of that happening. She knew her mother too well.

Lucy made it to the seclusion of her bedroom and closed the door behind her. What was happening? Vicki lecturing her earlier and now, Cal? On Monday she would call the airline and change her flight plans. She needed to stay in her world of corrupt government officials. At least she knew where she stood with them and could defend herself.

* * *

Lucy wore a sundress and sandals for her lunch with Jerry on Saturday. She wasn't sure what it was, really. Did Jerry want to get to know her better or did he like her, as Vicki seemed to think and this was really a date?

Jerry was an interesting man, and Lucy enjoyed the meal and the conversation. After their meeting at his office, he already knew her history.

"Are you a native Texan?" Lucy asked.

"Yes, but I haven't always lived in the Houston area. I grew up and went to school in San Antonio. Then I graduated from law school in Waco."

"What brought you to Cypress?"

"I married while I was in college which wasn't wise, I discovered. We didn't see eye-to-eye on many things, and unfortunately, it ended in divorce. Thankfully, there were no children involved, although I would've loved to have been a father. I was devastated. I gave up my law practice and traveled around the country for a while. When I ran out of money, I happened to be in Cypress. I knew no one and had no connections. That's when I met Cal Frasier at a coffee shop of all places. He was my first client. We met at his kitchen table because I didn't have an office." Jerry laughed at the memory.

"Cal offered to rent a space for me to hang my shingle. Then he proceeded to send some very influential clients my way. He and Kathy invited me to attend church with them, and the rest is history as they say. I owe a huge debt to Cal for rescuing me physically, if you will. He pointed me back to God who rescued me eternally."

"I have to be honest, Louisa. I was pretty infatuated with you when we first met, and the more I knew about you, the more I wanted to be more than friends. However, when I spoke to Cal yesterday, I realized he is falling in love with you, and I would never do anything to get in the way of his happiness. He's quiet, shy and reserved, and he is truly a good man."

Lucy was trying to put the words quiet, shy and reserved together with the man who was kissing her neck when they went riding on Wednesday. She wondered if they were talking about the same person.

Jerry continued, "I don't know how you feel about Cal, but I would advise you to tell him everything you told me on Thursday. If he finds out from someone else, he will be terribly hurt."

"I don't expect it to be a problem, Jerry. I'm leaving the beginning of the week and won't be back until I have to show up for the adoption hearing. I appreciate your concern and advice and am flattered you wanted to be more than friends. I was intrigued by you, also, when we met on the plane. Perhaps in another time, we could explore the possibility, but right now, I have too many things happening in Chicago, and I need to return before they spin out of control."

She thanked him for lunch and started to go. She turned back to him, "Cal and I had a remarkable few days, but I don't think either one of us believes love was part of the equation."

As she walked to her car, she talked aloud to herself. "What the hell are you talking about? Lucy Mae? You don't think love was part of the equation? Really? What exactly is the feeling you have every time you see Calvin Frasier? Strictly lust instead of something more? You need to go home to your house in Batavia, where you're safe from all these thoughts and feelings."

* * *

Sunday morning, Vicki drove her car to the church located on the south side of Cypress. Neither she nor Lucy said more than a few words. The nightmare was back again last night, but the list of whom it might represent was growing.

When Cal entered and sat next to Lucy, Vicki shot him a look of contempt.

Cal's son, Ben, and a pretty young woman Lucy assumed was his girlfriend, sat on the other side of Cal.

Lucy had attended church every Sunday for her entire childhood. Most of the hymns this morning were familiar to her with a few contemporary ones thrown in. When the congregation sang *Amazing Grace*, Cal's deep voice sounded soothing next to her.

When exactly had she decided to stop praying and reading God's word? After John died and left her to raise two children by herself or when Grandma and Grandpa died in the same year or when she realized her beloved ranch was gone or when the con artist she married took a large chunk of her assets? She couldn't remember but she did miss the comfort of feeling God's arms around her like her human father had put his arms around her when she was little. Would she ever feel that again? God's grace was amazing but was it intended for her? Her list of trespasses was pretty long.

When the service was over, they all walked out together. Cal introduced Vicki to Ben and Candy. Vicki introduced Lucy to the minister.

Ben spoke to Lucy. "My sisters and I would like you to join us next Saturday at the ranch for a cookout. Vicki, you are welcome, too."

Cal suddenly looked like a man about to have a heart attack.

"What? I mean, no one told me about this," he stammered.

"Thank you Ben and please thank your sisters for me, but I will have to miss it, I'm afraid. I will be back in Chicago by that time. If I can get a flight, I will be leaving on Tuesday or Wednesday."

Cal and Vicki both turned to look at her in disbelief. Before either one could say anything, Lucy offered an explanation.

"I need to get back. There are deadlines and some things going on I need to take care of."

She walked to the car, leaving Cal and Vicki standing next to each other.

"I know who you are, Mr. Calvin Frasier, and if you don't tell my mother the truth about a lot of things, I will," she said through clenched teeth. "You have until she gets on that plane, or I will make sure she knows everything about you."

She turned and joined Lucy in the car.

* * *

Leon called his sponsor. "Can we meet at the usual coffee shop, Frank? Say, in 30 minutes?"

Frank was there early. "Hey, Leon, what's up?"

"I called my sister."

"And...how did that go?"

Leon shook his head. "Not well, I'm afraid. She hung up on me, in fact."

"Did you get a chance to explain any of the circumstances surrounding the sale of the ranch?"

"I tried, but she wouldn't let me. I don't think she even heard me say I was clean and sober and no longer gambling."

"Listen, Leon. You tried. That is all that's required of you. Some people simply can't forgive; the hurt is too deep. You have asked God for forgiveness, and you know he has forgiven you. He's blessed your efforts to live a life far removed from your former one. You can't force your sister to accept your apology. She may never forgive you, but that is on her, not you. Do you understand that?"

Leon nodded. "But I want her to forgive me. I want her in my life again, even if it's a little bit. I would do anything to make that happen, Frank."

"I know you would, Leon, but as they say, 'The ball is in her court.' You've done your part; now leave it in God's hands. You never know how he may work things out."

They chatted about other things for a while, then parted ways.

"God, I know Frank says I don't have to try again, but you and I know I can't let go of this until I speak to Lucy, face to face."

CHAPTER 11

LUCY'S SON, PAUL, collected the children, Annie and Jarrod, from their respective Sunday School rooms. They joined their mother, Lynne, in the front of church.

"Isn't it wonderful God gave us such pretty weather for our bicycle ride today, Mommy?"

Annie skipped ahead of everyone else. She could hardly contain her excitement. This was the first family bike ride since she could ride without training wheels on her bike.

"Yes, Sweetheart. We do have to go home and change our clothes first."

"And eat lunch." Jarrod was only 8, but as a growing boy, his stomach often ruled his actions.

"Let's see, maybe after lunch, we should all take a nap," Paul teased and winked at Lynne.

"No, Daddy, not today. You promised right after lunch, remember?"

Paul helped Lynne put the finishing touches on their meal. The roast, potatoes and carrots had been in the slow cooker since early morning. He made a salad while Jarrod set the table and Annie placed the napkins by each plate.

"Can I say grace today?"

"Yes, Annie, you may."

Annie folded her hands and closed her eyes.

"Dear Jesus, thank you for our food and for sunshine and for our bikes and please bring Grammy home safe. Oh, I forgot…thank you for me not needing my training wheels any more. Amen"

After dinner, they put the leftovers in the refrigerator but decided they would take care of the dishes later.

"Do you both have your helmets?"

"Yes, Daddy. When I talked to Grammy, she reminded me to wear mine."

"Here, Mommy, let me help you fasten yours," Paul said as he grabbed a quick kiss from Lynne.

"Okay, kids, listen up. We're going to ride on the street to the park. We need to stay in single file and look ahead of where you are riding. Mommy will go first, then Jarrod, then Annie, and I will be last in line. Does everyone understand? No swerving or acting silly while we are in the bike lane. When we reach the park, we will ride the bike path and we won't have to watch for cars."

"Here we go," Annie shouted.

It was a sunny but cool day, perfect for riding. The leaves were beginning to change colors, and the smell of fall was in the air. They rode to the park and around the path. They stopped to rest for a few minutes.

Paul looked at their flushed faces. "I have an idea. Why don't we stop at the ice cream shop? We can get small cones and eat them before we head home."

"Oh yes, Daddy. Let's do."

They left the park and were again on the street in the bike lane.

"Look at those red leaves," Annie said as she turned her head to look over her shoulder at a tree. She also turned her handlebars and swerved out of the bike lane.

The sun bouncing off the truck's windshield blinded Paul as he looked toward the sound of screeching metal.

"Annie," Paul screamed as he saw the truck hit his daughter and send her and her bicycle into the air.

He heard the squeal of brakes, smelled exhaust fumes and heard car doors slamming as people stopped.

He ran to her but was afraid to move her. She lay in a jumbled heap of twisted bicycle frame, her left leg bent at an inconceivable angle. Lynne joined him on the other side, screaming for someone to call 911. There was so much blood he couldn't tell where it was coming from. He knew from many CPR courses that he should not move Annie, but he couldn't let her lay in the street and die. He heard Jarrod crying in the background and briefly saw a woman hanging on to him and talking to him. He also heard the sirens in the distance. He heard Lynne praying. Everything seemed to be moving in slow motion, and he was powerless to do anything. The world stopped.

The paramedics loaded Annie on a board and slid it into the back of the ambulance. Lynne climbed in the back with her while Paul scooped Jarrod up and ran home as fast as he could. He vaguely remembered someone saying they would take care of all the bicycles.

"Is she alive?" he shouted to Lynne as he raced into the emergency room dragging Jarrod by the hand.

Lynne nodded but couldn't speak. Jarrod clung to his hand, tears continuing to run down his face.

Paul was thanking God they were within minutes of Delnor Hospital in Geneva. Even though it had seemed like an eternity, it only took a few minutes to get Annie to the hospital. Maybe everything looked a lot worse than it really was.

A nurse ushered them to another waiting room. Their clothes were covered in Annie's blood. After a few minutes, a doctor came out.

"Mr. and Mrs. Newsome?" They both nodded.

"We have Annie stabilized for now. Miraculously, I believe only her leg is broken. The x-rays may show other hairline fractures, but the left leg is obviously broken in multiple places. She has many cuts and abrasions, which we can suture, but she has a lot of head trauma. She will need more tests and a brain scan." He paused, as if he didn't want to say more. "She is in a coma."

Lynne's knees buckled, and Paul grabbed her.

"I know it doesn't sound like it, but the coma may be a good thing right now. She is being taken for x-rays and further assessment. Then she will be returned to her room. If you live close, you have time to go home and change if you want."

"I'm not leaving here," Lynne said in no uncertain terms.

"I know, Honey. I'm not, either."

Paul called some friends and their pastor to ask for prayers and for someone to grab some clean clothes for him and Lynne. Then he called Lynne's best friend and asked her to come get Jarrod. Paul knew he would be taken care of and comforted at Shelley's home.

Next he made the hardest call.

* * *

Lucy stood at the sink, drinking a cup of coffee, deciding if she should try to change her flight reservation today or if it would be better to wait until Monday. She found airlines were usually better staffed on weekdays.

Before she could decide, her phone chirped. It was Paul.

"Mom." As soon as he said it, his voice cracked, and he couldn't continue.

"Paul? What is it? What happened? Take a deep breath and tell me."

"It's Annie, Mom. Hit by truck on her bike. In a coma. Please pray for her." He took big gulps of air between words.

Lucy covered her mouth so Paul wouldn't hear the panic in her voice. "I will be there, Paul, as soon as I can, okay, Honey?"

She hung onto the counter until she could steady her legs. *I have to get there...now.*

"Victoria," Lucy yelled. "Victoria, it's Annie."

Vicki came around the corner and into the kitchen.

"Mom? What is it? Who were you talking to?"

Lucy took a deep breath. This was not the time for panic. "It's Annie, Honey. There's been an accident. Paul could barely speak, but I heard truck, Annie's bike, coma and please pray."

Vicki grabbed Lucy's hands and said a prayer immediately. "I will call Pastor Kelly and he will tell the Prayer Chain."

They stood in the kitchen looking at each other in disbelief. Finally, Louisa said softly, "I have to get there. How am I going to get there?" She grabbed Vicki's shoulders and squeezed them, "How am I going to get there? Surely you know someone with a private plane don't you?"

Vicki called Jerry. She thought if anyone would know someone in the surrounding area, he would. She briefly explained the situation.

"Oh no, Vicki. I will call you right back; I may know someone. Please tell Louisa I will keep her and Annie and all of you in my prayers."

Fifteen minutes later, Vicki's phone rang.

"Cal has a friend who owns a Cessna 310. I remembered Cal mentioning it when he had this friend fly him to a cattle auction. He says it will take roughly four and a half hours. Perhaps your mother should try the airlines. That would be a shorter flight."

"She has been frantically trying, but with no luck so far. Did Cal say if the plane and pilot were available?"

"He was going to try and reach him. If there's a way to make it happen, I'm sure Cal will find it."

Vicki hoped Cal wouldn't refuse to help after the way she talked to him this morning after church. No, she might not care for the man any longer, but she didn't believe he would purposely be cruel to someone in need.

Vicki's phone rang a second time. It was Cal.

"Tell your mother to throw some things in a bag. I will pick her up in 30 minutes. Oh, and by the way, I'm going with her."

He hung up before Vicki could say anything.

CHAPTER 12

LUCY PACKED A SMALL bag, placed the revolver in the required locked box for transporting in a plane and added her laptop and papers. She dressed for what she knew would be a long four and a half hours. She could not believe this was happening. Perhaps this was the shadow over her shoulder in her dream…no, she didn't think so.

Cal arrived within 20 minutes.

"You must have set a new land speed record."

"Simon will meet us at Houston Hobby. It's the airport where he keeps his plane. Let's go."

Cal looked back at Victoria as he ushered Lucy out the door, but said nothing.

"I appreciate your friend taking the time to make this flight," Lucy told Cal.

"When I told him the reason you needed to go, he agreed immediately. Simon is a good man, with grandchildren of his own. He understood the urgency."

They were silent for much of the 45-minute drive to the airport. Because it was Sunday, traffic was light, which was in their favor.

Lucy glanced in the back seat of Cal's truck and saw another bag next to hers.

"If you're planning to go along, it isn't necessary. I can get to the hospital by myself."

"Lucy, you may be upset with me, and you do not have to speak to me on the flight, but there is no way I am letting you go home alone. You are understandably distraught, and whether you know it or not, you need someone with you. You don't have to be a pillar of strength every minute of every day."

"Thank you." She said it so quietly, he barely heard it.

Cal parked near the hangar Simon used and found plane and pilot ready to go.

"Simon, this is Louisa. Louisa, this is my friend and our pilot, Simon."

"Hello, Simon. I will never be able to thank you enough for doing this. I'm sure this wasn't on your agenda for a Sunday afternoon."

"I'm always willing to help a friend, ma'am, and Cal is a good friend. Let's get this bucket of bolts in the air."

Cal had stowed both bags while Lucy and Simon were talking. He had not seen Lucy this quiet since he met her. In addition to worry about Annie, Cal sensed anxiety about something else.

"Are you okay? Are you frightened to fly in a small plane?"

Lucy shook her head and then hesitantly explained, "My parents died in a small plane crash when I was 4. My father was the pilot. I have not been in one since."

She forced herself to climb in and fastened her seatbelt. Cal took the seat next to her.

You can do this, Lucy. You have to, for Annie, she told herself.

"Will you have to refuel, Simon?"

"We're going to try to make this a non-stop flight, ma'am."

"Can you land at DuPage?" Lucy asked. "It's the closest to Delnor Hospital,"

"Planning on it, Louisa."

Lucy closed her eyes and leaned on Cal's shoulder even though it was difficult with the space between the seats. She fell asleep for a while and then suddenly woke with a start.

"Cal, what if Annie dies before I get there?"

He had no answer for her, but held her as tightly as was possible inside the plane. Cal silently implored God to spare Annie's life.

*   *   *

Annie was still being tested and x-rayed. A uniformed officer arrived. He apologized for having to ask some questions at such a difficult time. Paul answered as best as he could. The policeman said the driver of the truck was definitely speeding in the residential area and was being tested for alcohol and drugs.

*   *   *

After he left, it seemed like hours before Annie was wheeled to a room in the Intensive Care Unit, which meant Paul and Lynne could go into her room only at designated times for a few minutes.

Friends from church and neighbors came by, stayed for a short time, prayed with them and offered to do anything they could. Shelley brought clean clothes when she picked up Jarrod.

Lynne suddenly jumped up. Her eyes were glassy. "Paul, the dinner dishes aren't washed. Remember, we left them. I need to go home and wash the dishes."

Paul grabbed Lynne as she stood. "You're not going anywhere, Sweetheart. The dishes don't matter." He knew it was Lynne's exhaustion and worry causing her to say delirious things. He held her and allowed her to cry until there were no more tears.

"What will we do if, if…Annie…"

"Shhhh, it will be all right. God has his arms around our little girl."

*   *   *

Simon was determined to make it to DuPage Airport without taking the time to stop and refuel. He had gone farther on just one tankful, but there was a little more wind resistance today. He kept an eye on the gauges.

Cal knew enough about planes to realize they were going to be cutting it close on the fuel, but he trusted Simon. His friend had been flying for years. Before he owned his own plane, Simon was a helicopter pilot in the service. Simon had made it through some harrowing experiences, and Cal knew if it could be done, he would do it.

He looked at Lucy resting on his shoulder. She had only spoken a few words since they left Hobby Airport. He wished he knew what she was thinking, but he remained quiet.

He had no idea what he was going to do when they arrived, but he knew he couldn't allow her to go to the hospital by herself, even though hospitals made him extremely uncomfortable. He had not been in an actual hospital since Kathy died, choosing the smaller rapid-care places if he needed any stitching or meds, which was seldom.

The words and images all ran together in his mind: *tests, radiation, chemo treatments, hope, mastectomy, more chemo, death.* Kathy died 10 years ago, but when he entered a hospital, he relived the entire scenario.

Simon glanced at Cal over his shoulder and shook his head slightly.

"Gonna' be close, Pardner."

The lights of the airport runway came into view, not a moment too soon. Simon landed the plane with one engine sputtering due to lack of fuel. Simon and Cal both breathed silent prayers of thanks.

Lucy sat up and reached for her bag. "How much do I owe you, Simon?"

He smiled. "Not a thing. It's been taken care of. You go give that little girl a hug from me. When she's all healed up, you tell her I promise her a ride, okay?"

"I will tell her. Thank you again. You have my undying gratitude."

Cal called a cab. It arrived almost immediately. A few minutes later, the driver dropped them at the hospital. Cal kept his arm around Lucy's waist to keep her from falling over.

"Where do we find the ICU and Annie Newsome?" Lucy asked at the information desk.

"That would be on the second floor. But only family can be in that area."

"I'm her grandmother, and this is my husband."

As they walked to the elevator, Lucy smiled a bit for the first time that day.

"I know that was a lie, but I'm too tired to explain it to anyone."

* * *

Victoria called David and explained what had transpired during the day.

"I'm coming home. My work here is nearly finished, and someone else can do the presentation tomorrow. I want to be there with you, Vicki."

"I need you to be here, David, for lots of reasons. I'll explain when you get here. Be safe. I love you."

* * *

Lucy embraced Paul and Lynne at the same time. The three of them stood together, arms around each other, looking through the window at Annie. "Is there anything new?"

Lynne shook her head.

Paul turned to Cal, acknowledging his presence in the room. He was surprised at the man's height and broad shoulders. He nearly filled the small room.

"You must be Cal. I'm Lucy's son, Paul. How can we ever thank you for bringing Mom on such short notice?"

The two men shook hands.

"There's no need to thank me. I happened to know a man with a plane. That's all."

Lynne wrapped her arms around Cal and hugged him. "Thank you. When Annie wakes up, she will want to see her Grammy, and you made that possible."

They couldn't go into the room where Annie was stretched out on the bed, but could see her through the large glass window. Annie looked so tiny lying there. Her left leg was wrapped and in a sling of some sort. Her head was nearly covered with bandages, and she had tubes everywhere. She looked as though she was sleeping peacefully. The only sound was the beeping of the monitors and the soft whoosh of the ventilator that was breathing for her.

The hospital provided a room with a bathroom and two beds for Paul and Lynne to use.

"You two go get some rest, even if you don't sleep. Cal and I will stay here and let you know if anything, no matter how slight, changes."

After some protest, Paul managed to persuade Lynne to come with him and lie down for a few hours.

Lucy sank into the recliner. Cal sat in the other chair, stretched his long legs and propped his feet on the footstool.

"Who would ever have thought a normal day could go so terribly wrong?" Lucy observed.

"This morning does seem like a long time ago, doesn't it?" Cal said.

"It makes me realize we are never promised tomorrow. We only have today, and we should make good use of it. Let the people we love know about it instead of waiting for some sign in the sky or something."

"When I get home, I'm going to make sure I see my grandchildren more than once a month," Cal promised himself.

"Cal, tell me something. Did you want to kiss me on our first date or did you kiss me because I asked you to? And did you even want to go on that date? I asked you, if I remember correctly."

Smiling, he answered, "Lucy, I wanted to kiss you the first time I laid eyes on you, and if you hadn't asked me for a date, I was going to ask you. You beat me to it. Why are you asking?"

"Vicki accused me of acting like a love-struck teenager. She seems to think I forced you into things. She seemed awfully cold to you this morning, too. Perhaps she thinks we should both act our age."

"Maybe she is angry with me for taking some of your time while you were there to visit her."

"That would be selfish and petty, wouldn't it? No, I think there's something else bothering Vicki. I overheard her talking to David when she thought I was out of the room. I couldn't hear everything she said, but I did hear Montgomery County Land Office. I can't imagine what she would want there."

Cal said nothing. This was not the time. He would wait until Annie was better before he confessed to Lucy. Unfortunately, then he would probably be shut out of her life forever.

They both dozed off but woke immediately when the quiet was broken by alarms of all kinds.

"Get Paul and Lynne," Lucy told Cal as she jumped from the chair.

Nurses and a doctor rushed through the door. They transferred Annie to a gurney and hurriedly pushed it out to the hall.

"What's happened?" Paul asked breathlessly when he and Lynne charged into the room.

The doctor explained, "Annie's breathing became erratic which sounded the alarm. She may have fluid collecting on her brain. That's always a possibility with the type of concussion Annie sustained. If that's the case, she will require surgery to relieve the pressure."

CHAPTER 13

THE SURGEON TOLD THEM it could be five hours before Annie would be back in her room in the ICU.

They all found a chair in the waiting room, but no one could speak.

"Can I get coffee for anyone?" Cal asked. "It's going to be a long night."

He left to find the cafeteria. Paul looked at his mother and wondered about her relationship with this tall stranger. He smiled at his thoughts. *Tall stranger…boy, that was a phrase straight from an old-time movie.* He liked Cal, but this didn't seem like the right time to ask his mother about him.

"Mom, I want you to know how much you mean to Annie. She loves you, in her words, to the moon and back."

Lucy nodded her head and smiled. She didn't trust herself to speak.

She stood abruptly. "I'm going to find the hospital chapel. I'm sure they have one."

She followed the signs until she found the quiet little room. It smelled like lavender and there were a few battery-operated candles flickering. The seating consisted of three short wooden pews with a padded kneeler for each one. At the front was a painting of a cross with the scripture words from Psalms 34 reminding her how the Lord promises to be close to the brokenhearted and those who are crushed in their spirit.

Lucy pulled a kneeler down and knelt on it. She folded her hands and looked up at the cross. It had been so long; she didn't know if she knew how to pray.

"Father, I know I turned my back on you a long time ago, and I ask your forgiveness for that. Grandma and Grandpa would be so sad to think their little Lucy Mae no longer reads her Bible or prays. They never lost faith in your love and goodness even when Mom and Daddy were killed. I'm not that strong."

When Paul told Cal he thought Lucy was in the chapel, he went to join her. He heard her praying aloud. He stayed outside the door so he wouldn't disturb her.

"Please spare Annie, Lord. She's a sweet baby who loves you. She says her prayers and knows all the Bible stories. I've heard her talk to you as though you are her best friend. Please don't punish her and Lynne and Paul because of my sins. Punish me, not them. Please, Father, please."

Lucy put her head on the back of the pew in front of her and cried so hard her shoulders were shaking. Cal couldn't bear to see her like that. He slid in next to her, wrapped his arms around her and held her until there were no more tears, only exhaustion. They sat like that for a long time. Finally, Lucy sat up and wiped her face.

"We had better get back to the waiting room before they send the St. Bernards after us."

* * *

"Mom, why don't you and Cal go home for a bit? You can see Jarrod at Shelley and Mike's house. Lynne and I aren't going to leave until Annie is out of surgery."

"Are you sure, Paul? I came to be with you and Lynne and Annie. I don't want to leave."

"I know, but Jarrod needs you, too. Please tell him Mommy and Daddy love him."

Lucy hugged Paul and whispered, "I love you so much. We will be back soon. Call if they bring Annie back sooner."

As they walked down the corridor, Lucy realized they wouldn't be able to see Jarrod. It was now the middle of the night, and the Smiths would be in bed. Somewhere they had all lost track of time.

"Let's get a cab. We'll go to my house for a shower and change of clothes. Maybe we can see Jarrod in the morning before we go back to the hospital."

When the cab stopped in front of her house, Lucy breathed a sigh of relief.

"Come on, Marshal. If any of the neighbors are up this late, you being here will give them something to talk about."

Cal chuckled and thought again how much he enjoyed being with this woman.

*   *   *

Lucy unlocked the front door and turned off the security system. She led the way up the stairs. "You can have the room I reserve for all my overnight male visitors," she quipped.

She opened the door to a large bedroom with a four-poster bed. The comforter and drapes were camel-colored and the large rug on the polished wooden floor was navy blue. There was an adjoining bath, decorated in the same colors.

"I'll take it. I was afraid it might be covered in pink ruffles or something equally girlie."

"That's the next bedroom. Annie chose the décor for that one."

At the mention of Annie, a shadow crossed Lucy's face.

"I'm going to take a shower and change out of these sweats. I don't think I can sleep, but you are welcome to."

She turned and disappeared into another bedroom. Cal knew his head was warning him about the thoughts that were running through it. He closed his door and headed for the shower.

The hot water felt good on Lucy's skin. She thought she was all cried-out but every time she thought of Annie and the possibility of never holding that smiling angel in her arms again, she cried some more.

Okay, Lucy Mae, get a grip on yourself. You will need to be strong for Jarrod and Paul and Lynne. What comfort can you be if you dissolve into a puddle of tears every five minutes?

She towel-dried her hair, ran a brush through it and slipped into a pair of light blue silk pajamas. She decided to go to the kitchen and fix a cup of tea and a piece of toast. It had been a long time since she had eaten anything. She couldn't sleep anyway.

While she waited for the water to boil, she looked for a loaf of bread in the freezer. She had thrown it in there before she left for Texas so it had to be there somewhere. When she found it, she pried off a slice and dropped it in the toaster. As she reached for a mug, Cal entered the kitchen, wearing a pair of cotton pajama pants but no shirt. When Lucy glanced at him, she nearly dropped the mug onto the ceramic kitchen floor.

Cal grinned sheepishly. "Sorry. I packed in a hurry; guess I forgot the shirt."

"I guess you did."

She would have to remind herself not to get involved. It would never work. She belonged here and he belonged in Texas. He would leave in a few days. Vicki was right; it was a "summer-camp middle-school romance."

Cal looked at Lucy with undisguised admiration in his eyes. She was wearing no make-up, no jewelry, her hair was still damp and he thought she was possibly the most beautiful woman he had ever seen. His good sense kept him rooted to the spot, but he was having a hard time keeping his thoughts in check.

"Would you like a cup of tea or a piece of toast? My refrigerator shelves are bare. I made sure I emptied them before I left. There's probably something in the freezer if you're hungry."

Cal finally found his voice. "I'm not much of a tea drinker, but since you have the water boiling, I'll have a cup with you."

They sat on opposite sides of the kitchen island, stirring the hot tea but not speaking.

"We probably should try to sleep for a few minutes. It will be another long day tomorrow or... has tomorrow become today? I'm afraid if I allow myself to fall asleep, I won't wake up until tomorrow night," Lucy said.

"Lucy, the words you spoke in the chapel…I couldn't help overhearing your prayer. Annie's accident isn't because of anything you've done. God doesn't work that way. Annie's accident was just that…an accident. God isn't punishing her because of your sins."

"I pride myself on being tough and able to take care of things. None of that matters now. None of those things will help Annie. I feel so helpless, Cal."

He moved around to her side of the island, took her in his arms and kissed her like he wanted to since they left the airport in Texas. If her return kiss was any indication, she felt the same way. She laid her head on his chest and relaxed her whole body against him. He wanted to hold her all night but didn't want to take advantage of the exhaustion and vulnerability she was feeling.

Lucy drew back and looked up at him. Cal placed his hands on the sides of her face, slid them down her neck and onto her shoulders.

"Don't stop," Lucy whispered.

The silk pajama top slipped off her left shoulder, exposing the top of the yellow rose tattoo.

He winced when he saw it and dropped his arms to his sides. Cal knew this was not the perfect time, but if he didn't say something now, he would lose his courage.

"Lucy, I have to tell you something..."

Lucy's phone chirped; she grabbed it and read the message.

"Annie's out of surgery. I want to go back. You can stay and get a good night's sleep, if you want."

She started for the stairs and then turned to Cal. "What were you about to say before the phone rang?"

"I wanted to tell you being alone with you is way too dangerous, Lucy. We need to go back to the hospital where there are other people. I can't trust myself to be alone with you. I'm sorry."

She nodded her head, knowingly. "I guess Paul called in the nick of time, before we did something we would both regret."

Lucy knew Cal was right. Still, she wanted him to hold her tonight and every night for the rest of her life.

What was she thinking? She had more self-control when she was 20 years old and in college, she scolded herself. It was time to put the brakes on this relationship; it could never work.

CHAPTER 14

LUCY GRABBED A LIGHT jacket and tossed her car keys to Cal. "Will you drive? I'm too tired."

Cal adjusted the seat to accommodate his long legs and eased the Lexus into the street. Lucy obviously had excellent taste in cars, as she did in everything else.

In a few minutes, they were at the hospital. Parking spaces were plentiful this early in the morning, making a short walk to the doors.

Lucy was asking questions before she even said "hello" to Paul and Lynne. "What did the doctor say about the surgery? It didn't take as long as he thought it would. Is that a good thing?"

Paul nodded. "The surgery went well. They are going to keep Annie in a medically induced coma for a few days so her body can rest and heal."

"Thankfully, there were no more broken bones, just the left leg. But it is broken in three places. Obviously that's where the truck struck her. If she hadn't been wearing a helmet, she would have most likely died from the blunt force trauma of hitting the cement sidewalk."

"The doctor says she has her youth and her strong, healthy body on her side in this battle," Lynne added.

"Paul, please take Lynne home for a few hours. We will stay right here. You can be back in 10 minutes if you need to be. We couldn't see Jarrod last night. It was too late. Perhaps you can pick him up this morning. I'm sure he won't want to go to school, anyway."

Lynne protested, but Paul convinced her it would be best. They reluctantly left the room and drove home.

When Lucy thought Vicki would be awake, she called to report on Annie's surgery.

"I'm thankful you called. I couldn't sleep last night thinking about her and praying for Annie and Paul and Lynne. By the way, David is flying in today. He said to tell you 'hello' and he's sorry he missed you this time, Mom. I'm sure you'll be back. Jerry said there might be an adoption meeting with the court in the next month. You may be required to be there. He will let us know in plenty of time for you to purchase a plane ticket."

"Okay. Let me know and I'll be there. I love you, Victoria. Oh, and tell my favorite son-in-law I love him, too. One more thing…I left the keys to the rental car on the desk. Would you or David return it for me please?"

"Yes, of course, Mom. Don't worry about the car. Just concentrate on what's going on there, okay?"

Lucy answered, "I will do that. I'm waiting for Cal to come back, so I will say good-bye."

Cal returned from the cafeteria with two steaming cups of coffee and two Danish rolls.

"Mmmmm, you certainly know the way to this girl's heart, Mr. Frasier. I love Danish rolls even though they're terrible for me." She paused before continuing, "Maybe that's why I'm attracted to them."

Cal smiled and winked at her. "Maybe."

"When I'm done with this coffee, I'll call the airline and book a flight for tomorrow. I think it's time for me to get back home. I still have a ranch to run."

"I'm certain Ben is missing your help. I appreciate everything you've done. At least, let me buy your ticket. You wouldn't be needing one if it weren't for me."

"Lucy, please. I'll buy my own ticket. As I recall, you didn't ask me to accompany you; I insisted."

Cal left the room to make the arrangements. He was back shortly.

"The only flight available isn't until Wednesday, I'm afraid. Something about a baggage handlers' strike."

"That's good. If everything is still quiet here, you can go downtown with me to my office tomorrow. I need to check on a few things. We'll surprise everyone. They aren't expecting me until next week. My office manager, Catherine, will absolutely die when she sees the cowboy I found in Texas." Lucy was laughing at the thought of Catherine blushing like a 10-year-old.

When she could go into the room again, she sat at Annie's bedside and stroked her hand. She sang the lullaby she used to sing to Annie when she was a baby:

"Hush, little baby, don't say a word. Grammy's gonna' buy you a mockingbird.

When that mockingbird won't sing, Grammy's gonna' buy you a diamond ring.

When that diamond ring turns brass, Grammy's gonna' buy you a looking glass.

When that looking glass falls down, You'll still be the prettiest little girl in town."

Nurses came in to check Annie's vitals, shooing Lucy out for a bit.

Cal cleared his throat. "Lucy, about last night...I want to apologize for being so bold. I meant it when I said I couldn't be alone with you. I haven't felt that way about any woman since Kathy died, and I wasn't exactly tactful about it. It won't happen again."

* * *

"Ben, have you told Dad about the cookout on Saturday?"

"Samantha, Lucy isn't here any longer. She won't be available for you and Jackie to hassle."

"She went back to Chicago? Woo-hoo. That's a good thing. Is Dad there? I need to talk to him, in case she comes back."

"Nope. He went to Chicago with her."

"What?" she spluttered. "What do you mean he went with her? For how long?"

Ben was enjoying this. "Don't know. Her granddaughter was in an accident, and Dad hired Simon to fly her back. He went with her. That's all I know."

"Have you talked to him? When is he coming home? I mean is he staying in a hotel or what? On second thought, don't answer that. I probably don't want to know."

"Oh, Sam, don't get your knickers in a knot. He called this morning. He'll be home on Wednesday."

"Well, we're still planning on coming to the ranch on Saturday. We need to have a family meeting. Jackie and I discovered some very interesting things about Ms. Louisa Crowder. Tell Dad to be there, OK?"

"I'll tell him. I can hardly wait," Ben answered sarcastically.

* * *

Vicki drove to the airport to get David when he arrived. As he pulled his bags to the passenger pick-up area, she ran to him, threw her arms around his neck and kissed him passionately. "I missed you so, so, so much."

"I thought I would never get back to you, Vic. It feels good to be in your arms again. Ahhh, Texas, home sweet home."

"I have so many things to tell you, David. You can't imagine."

"First, tell me how Annie is doing."

Vicki filled him in on the latest reports from her mother while they drove home.

Her phone rang. When she answered, she was surprised to hear her uncle's voice.

"Hello, Victoria. It's Uncle Leon. I'm sorry to bother you again. Do you know where Lucy is? I tried her home phone and her cell phone with no luck. Is she still in Texas with you?"

"No, she isn't. Paul's daughter was hit while riding her bike. Mom flew home to Batavia. She may not be getting good reception in the hospital or maybe she purposely turned it off while there."

"Okay. Thank you, Vicki. I will try to reach her."

* * *

Paul and Lynne returned in the afternoon. They both looked rested and better able to cope. They had made the necessary calls before they returned. They contacted Paul's employer, Jarrod's school, Annie's kindergarten teacher and Lynne's parents, who were on a cruise.

They brought Jarrod back with them. Even though they weren't sure he could handle seeing Annie, he insisted he needed to see her.

He stood thoughtfully observing Annie and the many machines hooked to her. "Is Annie dead, Mom?"

"No, Honey. She's sleeping right now, so her body can heal faster. One of these days, she is going to open her eyes and ask for her big brother." That seemed to satisfy him, but he couldn't take his eyes off her, as though he were willing her to wake up.

When the doctor made his rounds, he told them he wanted to keep Annie in the coma for several more days. When he was certain she would be able to breathe on her own, he would write orders for the ventilator to be removed.

"What happens after that?" Paul asked.

"We wait to see if she wakes up when her meds are gradually reduced. It's up to Annie's body after that, Paul."

* * *

Jarrod said he was hungry which reminded everyone it was dinnertime. Paul and Lynne decided they would stay with Annie in shifts. One would go home, get some sleep and when they returned, the other one would go home. Cal and Lucy volunteered to take Jarrod out to eat before taking him back to the Smith's house for another night.

Jarrod took Cal's hand as they walked down the corridor. "Mr. Frasier, do you always wear that cowboy hat?"

"Nearly all the time, Jarrod."

"I sure wish I had one."

"How about this? When I get home, I'll send one for you to wear. Would you like that?"

"Yes, Sir. All my friends will be jealous when I tell them I know a real cowboy."

Lucy lingered with Paul for a bit longer, sensing he wanted to talk to her alone.

"Mom, I feel a bit awkward asking this, but what is your relationship with Cal?"

Lucy smiled. "I haven't rightly figured that out yet, but I'll let you know when I know."

"Okay, I can take a hint. Mind my own business, right?"

"I was teasing you, Paul. I like Cal a lot, and I know the feeling is mutual. He's a good man, and we seem to have something between us. I'm just not sure what that something is."

"For what it's worth, Mom, this is my advice: if you have a chance to be happy, don't waste it. As we've seen this weekend, life can be changed in a second. I read a quote that was posted on social media last week. I wrote it down and put it in my wallet because I thought it was so true. I didn't know I would be reading it to my mother."

Paul pulled a slip of paper out of his wallet. "Here's the quote: *'No one is ever ready to do anything. There's almost no such thing as ready. There's only now, and you may as well do it now.'*"

"Thank you, Paul, for giving me that. I appreciate you not chastising me for being too hasty or too old to be interested in someone. Take care of Annie. I have a few business situations to address in the morning, but I'll be back in the afternoon."

As she walked away, Paul knew without a doubt who was giving her a hard time about Cal. It would undoubtedly be Victoria.

CHAPTER 15

AFTER EATING AT JARROD'S favorite place and watching him devour a cheeseburger, fries and milkshake, they dropped him at the Smith's house and returned to Lucy's home.

"Here we are again, Marshal...alone," Lucy said as they entered the house.

"You are so right. To avoid my having to apologize again tomorrow, I'm going straight to bed," Cal laughed.

"I would like to leave for the city by 8 a.m. If you want to come along, you're most welcome."

"Would you prefer I stay away from your work environment?"

"Not at all. You're welcome to ride shotgun any time."

"I'll set my alarm."

As they reached the top of the stairs, she turned to him and ran her fingers through the wisps of gray hair at his temples. "I'm going to miss you when you leave, Marshal." She stole a quick kiss and disappeared into her bedroom.

* * *

The alarm's jangling woke Cal from a sound sleep. He rolled over onto his back, trying to decide if maybe he did prefer to stay home, but knew he would miss precious time with Lucy, which he knew was coming to an end, for several reasons. He would have to tell her his part in the loss of the Yellow Rose before he left tomorrow.

When Lucy entered the kitchen, she smelled coffee. Cal was in the process of pouring a cup for her. "You're spoiling me. I could get used to a handsome man having my coffee ready in the morning."

Cal appraised her from top to bottom. "If those are your work clothes, Lucy, I want to work in your office so I can look at you all day," he told her as he shook his head.

It amazed him that it was possible for her to switch so comfortably from a jeans-and-boots-wearing gal into this high-profile, professional woman in dress clothes and heels. He definitely didn't know one brand of women's clothing from another, but he did appreciate a good-looking woman when he saw one.

"You look like a million bucks."

"Good. Because that's about what it costs to dress appropriately for the people I meet with," she laughed.

They finished their coffee and climbed into the car, with Lucy driving today. She maneuvered effortlessly through the morning traffic on the 45-minute commute to her office building.

Her phone beeped. She checked the number, put it on speaker and said, "Good morning, Phoebe."

"Good morning. Where are you and how is Annie?"

"I'm in the car, on my way to work. Annie is holding her own for right now. The doctor is keeping her in an induced coma so she can heal faster."

"Second question: how's Marshal Dillon?"

"He's good. He's right here. Want to talk to him?" Lucy winked at Cal.

"He's with you?" Phoebe spluttered. After a long pause, she continued, "Am I on speaker?"

"Yes, you are."

"Okay, Lucy. Very funny. I'll talk to you later."

"Bye my friend."

As she parked the car and turned off the ignition, Cal commented, "I admire you. I don't know if I could make that drive every day, especially in the winter, up here in the North Country." Lucy chuckled. "That's the beauty of being the boss; if it gets too bad, I work from home. Come on, let's surprise the heck out of everybody." She was grinning impishly, like a child enjoying a joke.

They entered a lobby that looked like something from a movie. Thick carpet, lots of glass, bronze fixtures, lush plants everywhere and richly colored furniture. Lucy stopped at a front desk to speak to a security person. He looked surprised to see her.

"Hello, Mrs. Crowder. It's nice to see you back. I wasn't expecting you until next week"

"I know. I had to change my plans. My granddaughter was in an accident, and I needed to come back early."

"I'm sorry to hear that. Is she going to be all right?"

"I believe so, but it will take lots of time. Frank, I want you to meet a friend of mine, Calvin Frasier. Cal, this is the best security man in the business, Franklin Kraft. I always know I'm safe in my office when Frank is watching the monitors."

The men shook hands. Cal could sense he was being appraised by Frank. He hoped he passed the test.

When they reached the third floor, the door to her office had the company logo on the outside—YR Industries. He had never asked the name of Lucy's company, but of course, the YR would stand for the Yellow Rose.

Her office manager, Catherine, did indeed turn 10 shades of pink when Lucy introduced her to Cal, just as Lucy predicted.

"Catherine, anything I should know, good or bad?'

Catherine's face registered a look of disgust before she said, "James is in your office. He's been in and out a lot while you were gone."

Lucy's face clouded a bit as she proceeded through the door into her personal office.

"Hello, James," she said as she walked through the door. A tall, dark-haired man Cal guessed to be in his late 40s spun around at the mention of his name.

"Louisa! Well, this certainly is a surprise. I wasn't expecting you."

She glanced at the sheaf of papers in his hand, took them from him and said, "Apparently not."

"James, this is my friend, Calvin Frasier. Cal, this is my business associate, James Roden."

The two men shook hands, each one assessing the other.

Lucy placed her purse in a desk drawer and her briefcase on the desk. She turned to Cal. "Make yourself comfortable. There are soft drinks, juices and water in the kitchenette behind you. Or, if you prefer something hot, Catherine makes a mean cup of coffee or chai tea, whatever suits your fancy."

As she opened her computer, she addressed James. "Give me updates on the Gerard Street project and tell me what happened at the council meeting last Tuesday. Did Jorgenson agree to our taking on the Florence Division houses?"

While Lucy and James discussed business, Cal surveyed the office. The plush carpet eliminated nearly all sound. The solid walnut woodwork and doors gave the room a warm feeling despite the otherwise neutral, almost austere furnishings. There were a few paintings on the walls but no pictures of family. He guessed Lucy kept her business and her family separate. There was an old photo of the ranch house located on the Yellow Rose property, with her company's logo beneath the picture.

Cal grabbed a juice from the small but fully stocked refrigerator. He pretended to read a magazine, but instead listened to the exchange between Lucy and James. It was obvious who was in control of the conversation but it was also obvious who wanted to be in control. Cal's gut instinct told him James was going to be trouble for Lucy, even if he had been a model employee in the past. When they were finally done with their business, James left the room. Lucy shut down her computer and turned to Cal.

"Are you ready for some 'on-the-worksite' time?" Lucy asked. She grabbed her purse, briefcase and the papers she had taken from James. On the way out, she handed the papers to Catherine and told her to shred them immediately. She repeated the word *"immediately."* Catherine took them and headed for the shredder.

When they reached the parking garage, Lucy pointed to a pick-up truck with the YR logo on each front door. "This isn't quite the same ride as my car, but it will do," she laughed.

She drove to a middle-class to lower-class neighborhood with construction materials piled in all directions and work trucks parked everywhere. Lucy parked the truck. She reached into the back seat, grabbed a pair of coveralls, pulled them on over her street clothes and traded her high heels for a pair of boots. She reached for a hard hat and handed one to Cal. "Regulations, my friend. Trade your cowboy hat for one of these designer numbers."

She walked confidently around the site until she found a burly looking older man. He grinned from ear to ear and gave her a hug. "Louisa. So nice to see you. The guys been askin' when you were comin' back."

"Anthony, I'd like you to meet Calvin Frasier. Cal, this is my number-one project manager and crew boss, Anthony Nichols. I can't imagine a project running smoothly without him. Are there any new developments I should be aware of, Anthony?"

"The third house in the row has more structural damage than we first thought. I'll run the numbers comparing the costs of making the repairs or tearing it down."

"When I get back to the office, I'll determine if zoning will allow a children's playground to be installed on the lot if it becomes necessary to remove the house. Right now, I'm going to check progress inside the houses that are nearly finished. You two can get to know each other."

Anthony watched her walk away. Without any pretense at small talk, he asked bluntly, "So, is Miss Louisa your girl?"

"I don't know, Anthony. I wish she could be, but I'm afraid it may not work out."

"She's one of a kind, Mr. Frasier. If you have any feelings for her at all, they better be honorable ones. Y'know, I work occasionally for a high-tech security firm but mostly, I've been in this line of work for 45 years, and I ain't never had a boss like her. At first, I wasn't too happy about taking orders from a woman, but that all changed once I met her. She's smart and tough, but she's also honest and fair and very hands-on. She even reads the blueprints to make certain it's all going according to plan. She pays well, provides benefits and will pay half of continuing education courses any of the guys want to take."

"And," he continued, "she never treats anyone like they're beneath her. About a month ago, I had occasion to go to her office downtown. Now that's a swanky place. She introduced me to people like I was somebody special or one of those guys wearing a suit and tie."

Anthony continued, "I do worry about her a bit. Like the rest of us, she's not getting any younger, and she needs somebody in her life, I think to protect her, maybe."

"Protect her from what or who, Anthony?"

"She's made a lot of enemies over the years. They all respect her, but some of them are pretty sketchy characters. She's been offered so many bribes she could have retired to some private island years ago. Some want her business and some want her, if you know what I mean. They're like piranhas, circling, just waiting for her to make a mistake. She'll tell you she's perfectly capable of taking care of herself, but I still worry."

*   *   *

When they were back in the truck, Lucy asked, "Did you and Anthony have a good chat?"

"Yes, we did. He certainly holds you in high regard, Lucy. He's pretty sure you walk on water."

She laughed. "He's a good friend. I would trust him with anything. Don't let him fool you with his 'good ol' boy' speech. Anthony is a college graduate and especially perceptive about people. He enjoys throwing everyone off by pretending he doesn't know which side is up."

As they drove back to Lucy's office, Cal reflected on the conversation. He also wondered what Anthony could possibly have been doing in Lucy's office a month ago, but he thought it would be wise not to ask.

CHAPTER 16

"I'M GOING TO CALL PAUL. Perhaps he and Lynne would like us to bring them some real food for dinner tonight. We can grab Jarrod, and we'll all eat at the hospital. I know…not too great, but different from cafeteria food, at least."

Paul agreed and was eagerly waiting when, armed with the goodies, Lucy, Cal and Jarrod arrived.

After dinner, they discussed the doctor's assessment of Annie's condition. It was still too early to tell how her body would react to the reduction of sleep-inducing meds. He wanted to start on Thursday.

"I'm taking Cal to the airport tomorrow. Can Jarrod go with us?" Lucy asked. "I know he should be in school, but I thought it might divert his thoughts from the situation here for a while."

Lynne gave her consent, and Jarrod was ecstatic.

"So, Cal, you're going back tomorrow?" Paul asked.

"Yes, I packed in such a hurry, I didn't bring many clothes. I think I've been wearing the same shirt for three days."

"You forgot a pajama shirt, too, as I recall," Lucy interjected.

Paul and Lynne exchanged glances, then in mock seriousness, Paul said, "Really? You want to expand on that statement?"

Lucy realized how it must have sounded. Trying to defend herself, she explained, "We were in the kitchen, OK? Sheesh, Paul, did I give you this much grief when you had a girlfriend?"

"I don't believe any of my girlfriends were standing anywhere without a shirt on," Paul answered, laughing.

Everyone had a good laugh, including Jarrod, even though he had no idea what was funny. It felt therapeutic to laugh, even if it was only for a minute. The past two days had taken a toll on everyone, especially Paul and Lynne.

Lucy sat at Annie's bedside for as long as she was allowed. After she lightly kissed her forehead, she and Cal took Jarrod home with them to spend the night.

The light on the answering machine was blinking when they entered the house. It was Vicki's voice: "Hi Mom. I tried your cell, but didn't reach you. Would you give me a call?"

Lucy climbed the stairs to her room to change into something comfortable. Jarrod wanted to show Cal his room, which was decorated in dinosaurs. He chose a board game they could all play and took it down to the family room. They played several times, with Jarrod winning most of the games.

Lucy stood and told Jarrod, "OK, you've beaten us enough times, young man. Besides, it's time for bed. If we're going to get Cal to the airport on time, we all need to get up early."

Lucy accompanied him upstairs, made sure he brushed his teeth and tucked him in.

"Wait, Grammy. Aren't you going to say my prayers with me?"

"How about this? I'll sit with you and listen while you say your prayers."

When she returned to the family room, she sat down next to Cal, tucking her legs beneath her.

"It felt good having you with me today, Cal. Sure you don't want to move to the North Country permanently?"

"Nope, never. But I enjoyed the day with you. I have to say, I am impressed with the scope of your business. I had no idea. I could use your skills running the ranch. Are you sure you don't want to move to the warmer climates of the South Country?"

"Maybe someday," she said rather wistfully. "Where I really want to move is closer to you, but we both know where that leads."

She suddenly remembered Vicki's call. "I'll be right back."

Cal couldn't hear Lucy's conversation, but he could tell by the tone of her voice, she was becoming more agitated the longer she talked.

Lucy stormed back into the room. "When will he give up? When will it end? He doesn't seem to get the fact I do not want to talk to him. Vicki is pretty sure he is flying here from Denver."

Cal stood and put his arms around her. "I assume you're talking about Leon. Maybe it would be a good thing if he came here. Then you couldn't hang up on him. You would have to listen to what he has to say."

She started to back away, her eyes flashing. "Whose side are you on? I don't ever want to see him again as long as I live. I want him to disappear. As far as I'm concerned, I don't have a brother. He died to me the night he signed the Yellow Rose away to some stranger."

Cal couldn't put it off any longer. Quietly, he told her, "Lucy, I am that stranger. I bought the Yellow Rose from Leon."

Her mouth opened, but no sound came out. When she regained her voice, her fists pounded on his chest. "Liar! You are a liar! And a sneak and a cheat. You could have told me. How dare you act like you cared for me when you knew how I felt about my home?"

"I didn't lie to you, Lucy."

"Not telling is the same as lying. You make me sick, Calvin Frasier."

He grabbed her wrists while she struggled to be free. "Lucy! Listen to me. There is so much more to the story of that night. If you would listen to what Leon has to say, you would know."

"Why should I hear it from Leon? Why haven't you told me the rest of the story?"

"I thought you and Leon should talk about it. It's his story to tell."

"What a stinking coward you are. No guts, no glory. I hope I never see either of you again."

"You can't always take the easy way out, Lucy. You shut yourself off from what you don't like or don't want to hear."

"Easy way out? You think I took the easy way out?" she hissed at him.

"You shut Leon out, saying you could never forgive him. Now you are shutting me out, unwilling to listen. You've shut God out. I heard you upstairs. You couldn't even say prayers with Jarrod. Have you ever thought perhaps you bear some of the guilt for what happened?"

"Me? How do you figure I'm guilty of anything? I was 1,200 miles away that night, and I sure didn't force him to drink or gamble or forge my name to papers."

"No, but you never came home to see if you could help him, either. You knew he wasn't good with the money end of the ranching. You took your half of the inheritance money and never looked back."

"Lucy, if you don't forgive, it will eat you up inside. Jesus took our place on the cross and forgives us for all the hurtful, stupid things we do, if we ask. Leon is asking you to forgive him."

"I hope God forgives you for what you did. I'm not going to. You can stay here for the night, but make sure you're gone before I get up in the morning. I'll tell Jarrod you said good-bye. Find your own way to the airport."

Cal let go of her wrists, and she stormed out of the room and up the stairs.

*   *   *

Cal immediately threw his things together and called a cab. When it arrived, he asked the driver to take him to the hospital and wait for him.

Paul looked up when Cal walked in. "Did you forget something?"

"No. I'm heading to the airport. I wanted to say good-bye and ask that you let me know when Annie wakes up. You have my number. I'll continue to keep her in my prayers. I'll make sure I send that cowboy hat for Jarrod." He glanced at Annie, so quiet and still. "I'll send one for her, too. It was nice to meet you, Paul. Please tell Lynne I said good-bye. You have a beautiful family. Take good care of them."

"Cal? Did something happen between you and Mom?"

"I guess you could say that. Do me a favor, if you would. If your Uncle Leon shows up, try to persuade her to listen to what he has to say, OK?"

He turned and walked down the corridor and outside to the waiting cab. He had never felt so old or so lonely in his life.

* * *

Lucy tossed and turned all night long, sleeping fitfully. Finally, she decided to get up and take a shower. Maybe she could wash away the events of the night.

Men, she thought. *Lucy, you have a gift for picking the rats. When are you going to learn? You told Vicki one of the things you learned from your disastrous second marriage was to fix any cracks you found appearing in the armor around your heart. You forgot this time.*

She felt sick to her stomach. She had allowed her imagination to run away with her. She had actually envisioned a future with Cal, thought she loved him and more importantly, she thought he loved her. She could still taste his kisses and feel his arms around her. Stupid thoughts.

She could take care of herself; she always had, and she always would.

Aloud, she said, "I guess when we were riding last week, I shot the wrong snake."

CHAPTER 17

CAL FOUND A SEAT at the airport and slumped into it. He tried to get comfortable but gave up. He had several hours before his flight and wished he could have said good-bye to Jarrod. He was a great little boy; he reminded him of Ben at that age. He would find Western hats and mail them to Jarrod and Annie.

He sincerely hoped and prayed Lucy would give Leon a chance to explain, if he did, in fact, arrive in Chicago. He knew he hurt her deeply by the things he said in anger. She hurt him, too, but he knew it was coming as soon as he told her he owned her childhood home. Perhaps he should have told her the entire story of that night so long ago, but he hoped if Leon told her, the two of them might be able to move on and start feeling like siblings again.

His heart hurt for what was lost. It didn't seem rational to think he was in love with a woman he knew less than two weeks, but he knew in his heart he was. There was nothing left for him now except to go back to working as hard as he had before he met Lucy, taking good care of the land, the stock and horses. He also promised himself he would see his grandchildren more often.

* * *

Lucy fixed breakfast for Jarrod. She wasn't hungry, but she sat with him and drank a cup of coffee.

"Where's Cal, Grammy? Did he sleep late? He's gonna' be in trouble. You told him to be up early, didn't you?"

Lucy smoothed his hair. "Cal had to leave early, buddy. He told me to tell you good-bye." Jarrod looked as if he wanted to cry. "He also said he would remember to send your hat, like he promised." That information perked him up a bit.

"Come on, let's go to the hospital. After lunch, we'll go to a movie, just you and me, OK?"

They left to see Annie. When they arrived, the nurses were checking her and changing her bed.

Lucy said she would stay if Paul wanted to get a cup of coffee before Lynne came to relieve him. Jarrod went with his dad.

"Did you know Cal went home, Daddy?"

"Yes, he stopped here to say good-bye."

"I really liked him. I think Grammy did, too, but they were mad at each other last night. I heard them from my room, but I don't know what they were shouting about."

"Sometimes grown-ups are worse than little kids, Jarrod. Maybe we'll see Cal again one day."

* * *

When Cal's plane landed, he retrieved his truck from where he had parked it on Sunday afternoon. Was that frantic flight really only three days ago? It seemed like an eternity. He called Ben and left a message.

"Ben, this is Dad. I'll be home within the hour. I'm coming to the ranch, not the apartment. I thought I should give you a heads-up."

When he wheeled into the long drive off the road and then into the circle drive in front of the house, he didn't know if he had the energy to get out of the truck. He skipped a shower and flopped across his bed. When he awoke, it was already dark outside.

Ben knocked on the bedroom door. "Dad? Are you okay? You've been asleep for hours. Dinner is ready, if you're hungry."

Cal rolled over and forced his body into a sitting position. He ran his fingers through his hair. He was sure he was a sight for sore eyes, but he didn't care. He joined Ben in the kitchen.

"Wow, Dad. You look like you were hit by a truck. What did you do? Stay up too late with Lucy?" he teased.

"Yeah, something like that, Ben." He pushed his plate back. "I'm not hungry tonight."

"That reminds me. I'm supposed to tell you the cookout is still planned for Saturday. I'm giving you a warning, but don't tell Jackie or Samantha I told you. They have been investigating Lucy. I think they have a whole list of reasons you shouldn't see her in the future. They will probably say all kinds of things about her."

Cal scooted his chair back and stood. "Not on my property, they won't." He left for the barn.

* * *

Jarrod chose the movie he wanted to see. Lucy bought him a soda and a bag of popcorn, even though she knew it would probably spoil his dinner. Jarrod laughed at the antics of the characters on the screen. Lucy didn't even see them; all she could see was Cal and how much he hurt her. When it was over, they stopped at his favorite fast-food restaurant. Lucy was amazed at the amount of food Jarrod could consume. She hoped he and Annie remained best friends forever. She remembered when she and Leon were young. They used to ride their horses everywhere together. They were best buds.

What happened? Even before that fateful night that sealed our separation forever.

Were Cal's accusations right? Had I deserted Leon when he needed me? I had a dying husband and two children to think about. I couldn't worry about someone 1,200 miles away...or could I have?

She was trying to justify her actions of nearly 25 years ago, but it wasn't working so well.

"Grammy? Grammy? Are you listening to me?" Jarrod's voice pulled her back to the present.

"I'm sorry, Sweetie. What did you say?"

"Are you mad at Cal? I thought you guys liked each other."

"We did, Jarrod. We both said some hurtful things last night." She smiled at him. "Cal had to go back to his home. He has cattle and horses he needs to take care of."

Jarrod's eyes grew wide with a new thought. "Do you think the next time you go to Aunt Vicki's house, you could take me along and maybe Cal will teach me to ride one of his horses?"

Lucy didn't foresee that ever happening, but she pacified Jarrod. "We'll see, Honey. Maybe."

* * *

Thursday morning, when Lucy stopped at the hospital, she learned the doctor had already made his rounds. Lynne told her the coma-inducing drugs were going to be reduced some. The doctor was hoping to remove the ventilator on Friday. If everything went well, Annie could then be moved to a regular hospital room.

Lucy drove into the city. She was useless sitting around at the hospital; it was time to get back to work, and the first item on her agenda was James. She never enjoyed letting someone go, but copying her account information was the final straw.

"Good morning, Catherine. Would you please ask James to come into my office? Thank you."

Catherine smiled to herself. Louisa didn't look happy, and Catherine wondered if she was going to fire James. She secretly hoped that was the case, as she had never liked him, but especially during the last six months. He seemed even sneakier than he had previously.

She adored Louisa and didn't want her to get hurt. Catherine was pretty sure James wanted to make Louisa his next conquest, but she knew that would never happen. Louisa was entirely too smart for that and much classier than James could ever hope to be.

It was rumored around the building that he had a gambling problem and quite a temper when he had been drinking. Of course, he never showed that side to Louisa.

"Please close the door behind you, James, and have a seat. I didn't want to embarrass you or my friend by causing a scene on Tuesday when we were here."

James interrupted, "You mean your cowboy, Louisa?" he asked derisively.

She refused to take the bait and continued, "Do you want to tell me exactly what you were doing making copies of my personal account information? How were you planning to use it? Who was paying you for those numbers?"

James lost his defiant look and tried another tactic. "Look, Louisa, I...uh...have a bit of a gambling debt, and someone was going to erase that debt if I gave him the information. But I wasn't going to actually give him all of it. Since I didn't give him any of it, can we just move on?"

"Someone? Does this someone have a name?"

When he didn't answer, she stood up and sat on the front edge of the desk, facing him. "I don't have time for playing 20 Questions, James. I have a pretty good idea which one of my competitors was bribing you. I figured that out the day Anthony told me you stopped the work on Gerard Street."

"Louisa, please, I can't lose this job. Haven't I done good work in the past, before this? I know I screwed up when I told Anthony to stop the Gerard Street work, but that was just one time. It would never happen again. And if you fire me, who is going to escort you to the charity events? We made a striking couple when I accompanied you to those shindigs, didn't we?"

"Yes, we did. However, you only agreed to attend those so you could let the media know about it and get your picture in the paper."

James ignored her comment and continued. "We could still be a couple, you know, a real couple. We would make a great team, Louisa. I would be much better for you than that hick cowboy you brought back with you."

Louisa controlled her urge to slap him.

Instead, she said, "James, you aren't worthy of holding that cowboy's hat."

She continued, "I'll have payroll cut you a severance check, but I'm sure you'll understand if I don't give you a letter of recommendation."

Lucy stood and walked back to her desk chair, dismissing him.

"You think you're so high and mighty. This isn't over, Louisa. I will get even with you."

"Save your threats, James. If I were you, I'd take my check and run, before I change my mind about giving you one. Believe me, better men than you have threatened me, and as you can see, I'm still here. You are obviously a lousy poker player, while I, on the other hand, am an excellent player, so don't call my bluff or I'll have you prosecuted for invasion of privacy."

James slammed the walnut door so hard the picture on the wall threatened to fall down.

Lucy leaned back in her chair and sighed. Maybe James had been the dark shadow hanging in the background of her dream, just beyond her vision. Or maybe it was Leon, who insisted on talking to her, or possibly it was Cal, who broke her trust and her heart. She smiled a bit when she thought how long the list of prospective shadows could possibly be.

Maybe it was time, as Grandpa used to say, *to get out while the gettin' was good.*

CHAPTER 18

LUCY WOKE UP FRIDAY morning knowing she needed some time with her best friend, but first she wanted to go to the hospital to see what was happening with Annie.

She left a message on Phoebe's cell. "Call me when you get a chance. I'll treat you to lunch; your choice of restaurants." That was a joke, as Phoebe was definitely a creature of habit and always chose the same little bistro for their chats.

"How's our girl this morning?" she asked Lynne when she arrived. When she looked in on Annie, it was obvious the early morning staff had already removed the ventilator.

Turning to Lynne, she grabbed her hands and said, "She's breathing on her own, Lynne. That's wonderful."

Lynne hadn't allowed herself to cry for several days, but now the tears slid down her cheeks. Lucy wrapped her arms around her. Lynne placed her head on Lucy's shoulder.

"Shhh, Lynne. I know you're exhausted. Is there something the doctor said that you're not telling me?"

"No, but...oh, Lucy, what if Annie never wakes up? I know she's breathing by herself, but some people never come out of a coma. What then? I can't bear to think about it."

"Then don't think about it, Lynne. Think about all the fun things you and Paul and Jarrod are going to do when Annie gets to go home. You are blessed by the many people, here and in Texas, praying for your family. God will honor those prayers, I know it."

Lucy asked herself, *Do you know that, Lucy? Do you believe what you just said or are you spouting words to help Lynne feel better?* She didn't know the answers to her own questions.

*   *   *

Cal promised Ben he would be back in time for the cookout on Saturday, although he wanted to be anywhere but there.

He saddled his favorite horse, Cutter, a muscular bay-colored quarter horse with black mane and tail. Cutter stood 16 hands tall and easily handled anything Cal asked of him. He tied a bedroll behind the saddle, dropped his rifle in the scabbard, checked his revolver and set off for some riding to clear his head. He wanted to be alone, but he did take his cell phone with him.

Times had certainly changed; there was a day when he would have set out for a week without any means of communication. He believed he preferred the way it was today, since dying alone in the far reaches of the ranch didn't hold much appeal for him.

While he was thinking about that, his cell phone indicated there was a message. It was from Paul. *Annie breathing on her own. Now we wait as patiently as we can. Keep praying she wakes up soon. Jarrod misses you.* That was good news and definitely an answer to prayers.

The air was becoming a bit cooler each day. Winter was coming soon enough. That thought led him to thinking about Lucy and her driving during the winter in Chicago. It seemed no matter how innocent his thoughts started out or on what subject, they always came full circle to include Lucy.

He had replayed their final hours together about 50 times in the last two days and had come to terms with the fact he would never share his life with her. He desperately wanted to, but he was a realist. She would forever tie him to the loss of the Yellow Rose and everything it represented to her. She would never be able to look at him without those thoughts going through her head.

He survived after Kathy died; he would survive again. This time it felt like *he* died. He rode with no particular destination in mind, stopping occasionally to give himself and Cutter a rest. When nightfall crept in, he built a small campfire, ate what he had packed and stretched his long frame out on the bedroll.

When he sat up in the morning, he knew why he didn't sleep under the stars any longer. His back felt every lump, twig and pebble that was under his blanket. *I am getting too old for this*, he told himself. He fixed his breakfast, rode for a few hours and then headed back to the house by a different route. He was anxious to see his grandkids today.

Jackie, her husband Gary and their 2-year-old son, Gabe, were the first to arrive at the ranch. Candy had come early in the morning to help Ben with the preparations. There were two picnic tables in the side yard, each covered with a festive plastic covering. One was to hold the food and there promised to be plenty of it; the other was for everyone to sit and eat and visit.

A little bit later, Samantha, Sean and their two children, Doug, 7, and Amy, 5 piled out of their van, lugging a cooler and a picnic basket.

Amy walked to the grill where Ben was preparing some steaks, "Uncle Ben, Mom says you're making steaks. Can you please make a hamburger for me? I don't like steaks so much."

"You got it, Amy. How about a few hot dogs, too?"

"Yes. Doug likes hot dogs."

When Cal came out of the house, Amy and Doug came running to him. "Grandpa! Hi, Grandpa."

He scooped Amy up in one arm while Doug walked beside him.

"I missed you guys. I haven't seen you for a while; I think you grew a foot."

Doug, who knew how long a foot was, laughed and said, "No, Grandpa, nobody grows a foot."

Gabe didn't come to him, but Cal went to him. "Hi Buddy. How's Grandpa's littlest cowboy?"

Gabe didn't speak but gave Cal a shy smile.

Dinner was delicious, but there was an ominous feeling hanging over the meal. When everyone had eaten their fill, discussed local news and events, the adults covered the leftover food and stored it in the coolers. Amy and Doug played in the yard while Gabe fell asleep on his father's lap.

Samantha spoke first. "Ben told us the reason you flew to Chicago was to escort a lady named Louisa. Her granddaughter was in the hospital?"

"That's right. Annie is the same age as Amy. She was hit while on a bike ride with her family. Her left leg is broken in three places, but the most serious is the head trauma. She was taken off the ventilator this morning but continues to be in a coma."

Sean shook his head. "That is scary. I tell the kids to always wear their helmets."

Cal nodded, "That's good, but Annie even had her helmet on. If she hadn't, the doctor said she would have died."

There was some discussion about the best type of helmets, but eventually, the conversation returned to his trip.

"Can I ask why you stayed for three days? I mean, once Simon got her there, why didn't you come back with him?" Samantha asked.

Cal looked at his eldest daughter and wanted to tell her it wasn't any of her business, but he didn't. Instead, he said, "Lucy was pretty distraught. I couldn't just shove her into a cab and wave good-bye."

"So, did you have the expense of getting a hotel room, too?" Jackie quizzed him.

Cal knew what she was really asking. "No, I didn't. Not that it's any of your business, Jackie, but I stayed at Lucy's house."

Cal took a deep breath. "I really don't appreciate this third-degree questioning. Would you like to know how many times I kissed her, too? Because I can remember every one of them. And, as far as I know, kissing isn't a sin. You may think I'm old, but I'm certainly not dead, OK?"

Ben looked at Candy for reassurance of what he was about to say. She nodded her head. He addressed his sisters. "I think you two are being ridiculous. What do you care if Dad likes Lucy? Are you afraid you might lose a few dollars' worth of inheritance when he dies?"

Jackie spoke up. "That's not fair, Ben. We don't care about the money or the ranch. We're just trying to protect Daddy."

Cal felt like he was in a bad movie, watching his children talk about him like he was invisible.

Finally, he held up his hand, "That's enough. I am 62 years old, which isn't exactly a doddering old fool. Lucy is 59. We are adults with all our faculties intact. I love her very much and would have asked her to be my wife, but the fact I bought the Yellow Rose a long time ago has come between us. So perhaps, all your meddling is in vain."

"You were going to ask her to marry you?" Samantha spluttered in disbelief. "How long have you known her, Dad? Two weeks? What kind of spell did she cast on you?"

"Sam, that's enough." Sean warned her.

"Yes," Gary agreed, glancing at Jackie. "Your dad is right. He has a right to live his life however he sees fit."

The sisters would not be deterred. "Well, did you know she owns a business that has houses in low income, dangerous areas of Chicago?"

"Yes. In fact, I accompanied her to one of the sites."

"Did you know she goes to parties and social events with a much younger man? Is she practicing to be a *cougar*?"

"Jackie, I don't even know what that term means, but yes, her business associate is James. She introduced us."

"Do you know how she got to be so wealthy?"

"Yes. A degree in business and lots of hard work."

"Okay, Dad, do you know she testified many times in the long trial of a drug lord who eventually was sent to prison? That means she had to be involved with his business somehow. And she had money from a trust long before she had the inheritance from her grandparents."

Cal knew nothing about the trust or the trial but he pretended he did.

"One last little bit of information. I'm sure you didn't know this, or at least I hope not, if you were going to marry her. Were you aware of the fact she never divorced her second husband? She's still married, Dad."

Cal felt as if Cutter had kicked him in the gut. He stood up, kissed his grandchildren goodbye and walked toward the barn.

Ben stood, also. "I hope you two are very proud of yourselves. You should mind your own business and let Dad take care of his. I'm ashamed of you."

Samantha turned to Sean. "Somebody had to tell him, right?"

Sean shook his head. "I agree with Ben. You and Jackie should have been happy for him and let it drop. He can take care of himself. Besides, we both know the information found in Internet records isn't always up to date."

CHAPTER 19

CAL BRUSHED CUTTER for a long time, trying to digest the things the girls told him. What trust were they talking about? While he realized he and Lucy hadn't known each other long enough to discuss a lot of things, it would seem like something might have been mentioned about sending some racketeer to prison. No wonder Anthony thought she needed protection.

If he was honest with himself, he didn't care about any of those things from Lucy's past, but still being married was a deal-breaker, even though there was no longer a deal to break. Lucy was still married? He was having a hard time wrapping his mind around that. Surely Paul and Vicki weren't aware of that or they would have told him when he showed an interest in their mother. Forget *them*…Lucy should have told him.

* * *

Lucy met Phoebe at her favorite place. They could sit in a corner and talk for hours without feeling rushed. The restaurant was never very busy, and they always left the server a nice tip for keeping their cups full and not interrupting their conversation.

"So, how is Annie? I think about her all the time. Poor kid."

"She is off the ventilator, but she hasn't opened her eyes yet. The doctor said it might take weeks. It will be such a relief when their life can return to some semblance of normal."

"Let me ask you something, Lucy. Despite my giving you grief about Cal, how do you really feel about him?"

"If you had asked me before Tuesday evening, I would've told you I was head over heels in love with him, but now I've regained my senses."

"What's that supposed to mean?"

"It means, Phoebe, Cal told me he owns the Yellow Rose. He bought it from Leon. Can you believe that? All these years of hating the person who swindled my brother, and I fall in love with him. Is that God's sense of humor or what?" she asked ruefully.

"That can't be true, can it? I mean, you would have known, wouldn't you?"

"How? I never saw Leon again. For a long time, I was too angry and hurt to check the records, and when I did, it was named the Benson Ranch, but no owner's name was listed. I should have checked further, but to what end? It wasn't mine so I didn't care who owned it. I had no reason to think Cal was the owner, but now I can put the pieces together. He introduced himself as Calvin B. Frasier. His son's name is Benson Frasier. Benson must be a family name."

"If you didn't care who owned it then, why do you care so much now, Lucy? It still isn't yours, so what does it matter?"

"It isn't so much the fact someone else owns it, but that Cal didn't tell me. Like I told him—not telling is the same as lying." She toyed with her napkin for a while. "In other news, I fired James yesterday."

"You did not."

"Yes I did. I guess this was 'National Get Rid of Unwanted Men Week.'"

"What did he do? Besides annoy the heck out of you, as usual?"

"While I was still in Texas, I suspected he was up to something, but I wasn't sure what. I had heard rumors that he had developed a huge gambling problem over the last few months. If the rumors were true, I knew at some point he would need money and become careless. When I had my accountant send my personal financial information and account numbers to an attorney in Texas for the adoption agency, I asked him to make 'dummy copies' with fake numbers and send them to Catherine, asking her to put them on my desk. Catherine had no idea what the papers were, but I walked in on James making copies of them. Busted. I even had Catherine shred them immediately so no one suspected anything."

"I'm tired, Phoebe. I'm not even looking forward to shopping for Christmas this year. I have no fall decorations up at my house. Thanksgiving might be turkey in the hospital cafeteria, depending on when Annie is released. Let's go on a cruise. My treat. What do you think?"

"I think you are trying everything you can to forget about Cal. That's what I think."

They talked for another couple hours, then went their separate ways. When Lucy came home, she thought she really should make an effort to get the fall decorations out. She couldn't think of any reason to do it this year. She curled up on the couch, covered herself with a blanket and fell asleep.

* * *

Cal attended church on Sunday morning, thinking worshipping might be the antidote for his depressed mood.

Pastor Kelley's sermon text was taken from Ephesians and spoke about being kind, tenderhearted and forgiving.

The sermon was exactly what he needed to hear. He had been asking himself what his response would be if Lucy did speak to Leon and decide to forgive the two of them. Could he forgive her for the hateful things she said to him? If he expected God to forgive him for his many transgressions, he needed to be forgiving, also. That included forgiving his daughters, too.

After the service, many people stayed for coffee and some socializing. Jerry found him and asked about Annie. Cal told him what Paul had messaged him yesterday morning.

"Jerry, I apologize for talking business at church. Do you have any free time at the office tomorrow? I'd like to talk to you about something."

"I'm sure I do. Let me check my schedule on my phone. Wait just a second, Cal. I need to speak to Victoria and David for a minute."

They both moved closer to the couple. Vicki was talking to a friend who had asked about Lucy.

"I'm sorry I missed your mother when she was here. I haven't seen her for so long."

Vicki flipped through pictures on her phone, found the one she was looking for and held it up for the woman to see. "This is what she looks like. Great picture, huh?"

"Wow. I'll say. Who is with her? They make a good looking couple."

Cal caught a glimpse of the picture Vicki was showing to the friend. He recognized Lucy and James. It looked as though James was wearing a tuxedo and Lucy was dressed in an evening gown. She was smiling and looked absolutely beautiful. Cal moved through the crowd, thinking he was going to be sick. If the picture was any indication, Lucy certainly wasn't sitting around pining over him.

Jerry found him outside. "I'm sorry about that. I was afraid I was going to miss them. They have an appearance in Family Court scheduled in a few weeks. I needed Vicki to let Lucy know so she can reserve her flight. Can you come to the office around 10 o'clock?"

Cal nodded. "Thanks, Jerry. See you then."

* * *

Lucy dressed, grabbed a jacket and drove to the hospital. It had been a week since the accident. Surely Annie would wake soon. This was so hard on everyone, Lucy thought to herself. Waiting was definitely not her strong suit.

Jarrod met her when she entered the room, "Grammy, Annie opened one eye, but she closed it again."

Lucy looked at Paul and Lynne. The smiles on their faces confirmed what Jarrod said.

"The doctor said that might happen many times before she is fully conscious. Isn't that wonderful? We are praising God for his many miracles and blessings."

Lucy volunteered to sit with Annie, so they could go to the cafeteria and have breakfast together.

Lucy stroked Annie's head where the bandages weren't covering it. "Sweetheart, Grammy needs you to wake up. I don't have anyone to watch *The Little Mermaid* with me." She put her head down on the bed rail and prayed for Annie, for her family and for understanding all the things that had transpired in the last two weeks.

She lifted her head when she heard a raspy, weak voice say, "Grammy, I did wear my helmet."

"I know you did, Annie. What a good girl you were to listen to Daddy. You have been very brave. I am proud of you."

Annie gave a weak smile and closed her eyes again. Lucy couldn't stop the tears; this time they were tears of joy. She could hardly wait to tell Paul and Lynne.

* * *

Leon had Lucy's address written on a slip of paper that he handed to the cab driver. When they reached her house, he said, "Wait for me. If no one is home, I'll need you to take me to the hospital, OK?"

He rang the doorbell and knocked several times. There was no answer. It was Sunday morning; maybe she was in church. He could have called, but knew from past experience she would hang up. It was better this way, face-to-face. What was she going to do? Shoot him? He suddenly remembered his sister was a much better marksman than he had ever been and that she carried a revolver with her at all times. That thought didn't give him much comfort.

"OK, let's try the hospital next," he told the driver as he climbed back into the cab.

When he got out, he paid the fare and sent him on his way. If she wasn't here either, maybe Paul would know where she was. He only had Vicki's phone number and had forgotten to ask her for Paul's. He took a deep breath and headed through the hospital doors and down the corridor.

*   *   *

When Paul, Lynne and Jarrod returned, Lucy was waiting to tell them Annie had actually spoken a few words. It was like birthdays and Christmas morning all wrapped into one celebration.

When things calmed down, Lucy excused herself for a minute. She needed to let Vicki and David know the good news. She walked down the hall, away from the noise. When she returned, she was still smiling.

She stopped dead in her tracks when she recognized the man in the chair next to Paul. He stood and came toward her.

"Hello, Lucy."

She started to turn back to the door. "Please, Lucy, don't go. Please hear what I have to say, and then I will disappear from your life forever if that's what you want."

CHAPTER 20

CAL ARRIVED AT JERRY'S office to find Jerry waiting for him.

"Good morning, Cal. What's on your mind this morning?"

Cal removed his hat and spoke quietly. "My daughters ambushed me Saturday evening. It seems they did a lot of research into Lucy's past. They thought they were protecting me, I guess, and since Lucy and I…well, we aren't seeing each other any longer…it was wasted effort on their part."

"First things first, Cal. Even though it's none of my business, what do you mean you and Lucy aren't seeing each other? What happened?"

"Long story, Jerry. I had to tell her I own the ranch that used to be the Yellow Rose, her childhood home. Let's just say, she didn't take that news well. She sent me home and said she never wanted to see me again. Pretty straightforward, don't you think?"

"I'm sorry, Cal. I know you cared about her. Maybe time and distance will heal the wound. She thinks you betrayed her, and that always brings intense emotions."

Cal chuckled a bit. "Intense might not be a strong enough word, in this case."

"I'll bet." Jerry hadn't known Louisa long, but he could imagine the fire in her eyes when Cal told her.

"I know it doesn't matter any longer, but I want to know how I can find details about some of the things the girls told me on Saturday."

"That depends if those facts are matters of public record or not. What did they tell you?"

Cal repeated the few facts he knew about the trial and the trust fund. He debated whether or not to ask about Lucy being married.

Jerry stood and looked out his office window. "Truthfully, Cal, I already know about those things. When Lucy came to give me her information for the adoption papers, we discussed many things from her past. She wasn't actually a client, but I would still consider anything she said as privileged information. For what it's worth, I wouldn't give it another thought."

Cal thought about that for a minute, then plunged ahead. "Did she tell you if she's divorced or not?"

Jerry looked at his friend and sympathized. "I really can't tell you that. If you want to know, you should ask Lucy. I'm sorry, Cal."

* * *

Lucy made the decision to hear what Leon had to say. There was no avoiding it, but it wasn't going to be at the hospital where other people could hear or in front of Jarrod, who had no idea what was going on. She told Leon to come to her house in the morning. Paul and Lynne offered to put him up at their house for the night.

* * *

When Paul dropped Leon off in the morning, Lucy asked Paul to stay. She needed a second person to hear this. After all, Leon's actions long ago affected Paul, too. Half of the Yellow Rose would have been his and Vicki's one day.

She made a pot of coffee and placed three cups on the kitchen island. She decided it would be the best place to talk.

She told herself, *It's close enough that I can reach across and strangle him if I need to.*

This was an awkward situation for all of them. There was no need for small talk; she wanted Leon to say what he came to say and then leave.

"Lucy, thank you for listening to me this time. I don't know your connection to Calvin Frasier, but he called me and begged me to tell you the events leading up to the sale of the ranch. I'm doing this for selfish reasons, too. I need to be able to forgive myself, and I won't ever be able to do that until I ask for your forgiveness."

Lucy looked at her brother with no emotion on her face. Leon looked older than his 57 years. His hair was thinning, and the lines around his eyes and mouth were deep. He had the look of someone who had lived an extremely hard life. *What happened to my little brother? The one who rode the ranch with me and picked wildflowers for Grandma?*

Leon took a swallow of his coffee and heaved a huge sigh. He seemed not to know where to begin. Paul felt sorry for him. His expression said this might have been the hardest thing he ever had to do.

"After Grandpa died, I was at a loss. I realized too late I should have paid closer attention to the things he was trying to teach me. I never had a business sense like you did, Lucy. I knew how to take good care of the land and buildings. I knew how to breed the best strains of cattle and horseflesh like the Yellow Rose was known for. What I didn't have was the 'take-charge' personality Grandpa did. No one would have even considered cheating him or not paying their bill. Because I was young, people took advantage of me. That's not an excuse, it's just a fact."

"I sold 100 head of prime cattle to a buyer in Houston. He never paid for them. I didn't have the gumption, intestinal fortitude, whatever you want to call it, to go after him. There were other deals that fell through. By this time, I'd run through all my inheritance money trying to make up for the losses and keep everything at the ranch running. I started to drown my sorrows in a bottle. First, I drank at home every night until I fell asleep or passed out. Of course, that meant I didn't function too well the next day."

"Calvin came over several times to tell me I had fences down. I told him to mind his own business. He could obviously see my life was a mess and the Yellow Rose was going to ruin. He'd tell his hired men to fix the fences because, of course, he didn't want his cattle to stray, and I think he genuinely wanted to help me somehow, but I rejected his offers of help. I was sure I could handle this and take care of myself."

"Well, that's one trait we obviously share, Leon," Lucy muttered.

"In this state of mind, I thought I could make up for the losses by hitting the poker tables. I went to the small clubs first, but then I gradually started going to the bigger poker palaces. Bigger pots, bigger payouts. Sometimes I won, but mostly I lost. Calvin showed up at the same table one night. Now that I can look back on it, I'm sure he followed me to try and keep me from getting in too deep. He played a few hands and then bowed out. He took me home and talked to me. He tried to tell me what he had observed while he was playing; several men were contriving how they could convince me to put the Yellow Rose up for collateral. I told him I didn't want his sermons, his God or his help."

"I couldn't figure out why he cared, one way or the other. I didn't find out until after the ranch was gone. Lucy, our Grandma Ivy's maiden name was Benson. She and Grandpa were second cousins. Her great-grandmother and our great-great-grandfather were siblings. When they first came to

Texas, the Bensons and the Hendersons purchased adjacent tracts of land. Through the years, there were no more Benson males to inherit the land, so it passed to Dwight Frasier, who was a grandson. He was Calvin's father."

"The land and heritage meant a lot to Calvin. He didn't want the Yellow Rose destroyed. A conglomerate from Dallas, calling themselves the Double K, had plans to carve it into 50-acre plots and develop it as a subdivision. The land would be covered with houses, streets and shopping malls."

"This continued for months; I won't bore you with the details. I barely stayed afloat, and any cash I made I gambled away, always sure I could win it back."

"I got in too deep, way over my head. The Double K had me where they wanted me. A huge—and I mean huge—debt, with no way to pay it, except with the deed to the Yellow Rose. I was told I needed to bring the signed deed. It seemed like the only way out to me. I forged your name, Lucy, and was ready to hand it over when Calvin entered the picture one last time. Against the wishes of his wife and the advice of his banker, he mortgaged his entire spread for the cash to pay my debts. The Double K men weren't happy, but he offered more than the amount of my debt, so they had no choice."

"He drove me home, and I handed him the deed. He told me I could stay and be a ranch hand if I wanted. I said I'd consider the offer, but in the morning, I packed a bag and left. I never came back."

Leon's coffee was cold, but he took a big gulp anyway. "I knocked around in Oklahoma, Kansas, anywhere I could find a poker game. Finally, I landed in Denver. Some Good Samaritan found me wandering on the street, suffering from hypothermia and delirious, and took me to the hospital. They treated me and sent me to a Christian shelter for homeless men."

"As they say, the rest is history. I went to sobriety meetings, stopped gambling, rekindled my love for the Lord and with his help, got my life in order. I've been sober and non-gambling for 10 years. I earned a degree in social work, have a job at the same shelter that helped me and I married a wonderful woman named Ginny, who loves me."

"As I said in the beginning, I don't know your relationship to Cal Frasier, but I had not heard from him until a few weeks ago. All he asked was that I tell you about that night. He didn't cheat you and me out of our home, Lucy. I'm the one who lost it. Cal saved it. He risked his family's home and every cent he had to save it. He leased the Frasier Ranch to a local rancher and moved his family and cattle operations to the Yellow Rose. It was renamed Benson Ranch for his great-grandfather."

"I hope you can forgive me. I wish we could be friends, as well as brother and sister, but I also understand if you say no. I really do. I'm proud of you, Lucy, and all you've accomplished."

Leon stood. "Paul, we can go now, if you're ready."

CHAPTER 21

CAL WALKED THE SHORT distance from Jerry's office to the Western Wear store. He purchased a black hat for Jarrod and a pink one for Annie. When they were packaged and ready for shipping, he realized he didn't know Paul and Lynne's address.

He called Paul. His voicemail picked up, so Cal left a message. He thought about dialing Lucy's number but decided against it. He could call Vicki, too, but he didn't think anything had changed in her opinion of him, so he forgot it. He told the woman who was helping him with his purchase, "I'll call back with the address. I can't seem to reach anyone right now."

He wanted to get the hats sent off. He didn't want Jarrod to think he had forgotten. His stomach felt like it had been forgotten. He drove to the Long Branch Café for lunch. As he sat at a table waiting for his food, he remembered this was where he first noticed the pretty woman with the dark hair. It seemed like years ago, instead of weeks.

* * *

"Mom, call me when you have time. Jerry has a date for the Family Court meeting. He said it would be the only time you would need to be here. We're so excited—it's getting closer! Talk to you later. Bye."

* * *

Lucy stayed seated after Paul and Leon left. There was too much information to digest immediately. She had been angry at him for so many years; she wasn't sure what she was supposed to be feeling right now. His flight back to Denver wasn't until tomorrow morning. They agreed to meet for dinner at a small restaurant in downtown Batavia, just the two of them.

Leon was quiet as they drove back to Paul's house. "Uncle Leon, I respect you for what you did today. I know it had to be difficult. I'm sorry for all the time Vicki and I missed getting to know you. I realize Mom didn't want to speak to you, but that's no excuse for us not reaching out. I ask your forgiveness for that."

"There's no forgiveness necessary, Paul. I should have contacted you. I guess we all owe a debt to Cal Frasier for finally forcing us to contact each other."

Paul wondered how his mother was going to fix her relationship with Cal now that she knew the truth. Then, again, maybe she didn't want to fix it or perhaps Cal didn't want to. Thinking of Cal, Paul dialed his number, remembering he had missed a call from him.

Cal answered after the first ring. "Hi, Cal. I'm sorry I missed your call. I turned my phone off while Uncle Leon and I were at Mom's house, talking."

There was complete silence on the other end. "Cal? Are you still there?"

"Yes, I'm here." He recovered his voice and said, "What I called for was your address. I'm shipping the hats for Jarrod and Annie and realized I don't have it."

"2214 Concord Avenue. The zip code is 60510. The best news is Annie has opened her eyes a couple of times and even said a few words to Mom yesterday."

"I'll make sure I tell everyone at church. They have all been praying for her." After a pause, Cal continued, "Paul, if Leon hasn't left yet... tell him I said thanks."

Cal's emotions were going around faster than a dirt devil in a Texas dust storm. *What happens now?* he asked himself. *Do I call Lucy or wait for her to contact me? What if she never calls? There's no guarantee she will forgive Leon or me.*

* * *

Lucy spent the afternoon trying to decide how she felt about Leon and the things he told her. She had no doubt it was all true. He wouldn't fly from Denver to tell a bunch of lies. She also had to sort out her reaction to his words and how they affected her relationship with Cal. Should she call him and apologize? What if he wouldn't accept her apology? She had been mean and unforgiving when she told him to leave. She still didn't understand why Cal wouldn't tell her how it all happened. Paul seemed to think that Cal hoped forcing Leon to tell her would fix their sibling relationship. Would he really put that above *their* relationship? She didn't have the answers, and she was getting a headache thinking about it.

* * *

Lucy arrived at the quiet restaurant before Leon. When he entered, he spotted her and slid into the booth across from her. They discussed his job and her business projects. Finally, Leon asked, "Lucy, I have to ask. How do you know Cal Frasier?"

"I met him when I visited Vicki and David a month ago. I know how crazy this is going to sound, but it was love at first sight. We had a natural attraction from the beginning. He flew with me when Annie was hurt and I needed to come back home. The night before he was going home, he told me he was the owner of the Yellow Rose. He wouldn't tell me the whole story, he just said that was up to you."

"I said some terrible things to him, Leon. I don't think he'll ever forgive me. It makes me sad; I think I did love him. He told me that night I needed to accept part of the blame, also. I wasn't there when you needed me. He told me I shut out the people who make me angry. I shut God out of my life, too. He's right."

"Listen to me, Luli. You couldn't have helped me, even if you had come back. I was in too deep. As far as shutting people out, we're all guilty of that. It's part of our sinful nature."

Lucy smiled. No one had ever called her Luli except Leon when he was very young. Later he changed it to Lucy.

Leon continued, asking earnestly, "Where do you stand in your relationship with God, now, Lucy? Still shutting him out of your life?"

"I've been doing a lot of soul-searching since Cal told me those things. I've tried to discover why the Yellow Rose means so much to me. Why I was obsessed with thoughts of it. I think John dying, Grandma and Grandpa dying, struggling to raise the kids by myself, the environment of the work I do and the people I deal with every day, and then the *mistake marriage* I made all lumped together. I blamed God for allowing it to happen. In my head, the only sanctuary I ever had where I was truly happy was when we lived at the ranch. It became a symbol of all the things I didn't have any longer and you bore the brunt of my anger and frustration for taking that away from me. Do you think you can forgive me for that?"

"You know I have always loved you, Lucy. You were the cowboy Grandpa wanted, and I wasn't. You listened to everything he wanted to teach us. I had no interest in shooting at cans on fence posts, but you hit every one. I liked riding for fun, but you could ride like the wind with or without a saddle.

And playing poker...do you remember when you were 12 or 13 years old and the three of us were playing Texas Hold 'Em? Grandpa said, "I've got you now, Lucy," and put his cards on the table. You looked at him and said, "But Grandpa, I've got pocket aces." He laughed so hard he almost fell off his chair. He was proud of you, Lucy."

"I just wanted to raise the best cattle and horses in Texas, and I failed at that, too. But God has given me a new life, and I cherish every day of it. I want you to feel his love and forgiveness, too. You don't have to do anything. He is always waiting with open arms, Lucy."

Leon left for the airport after their lunch. Lucy offered to drive him but he said it was best this way. He put his hand out to shake her hand when Lucy hugged him instead.

*   *   *

Vicki called again. "Mom. October 20th is the date you will need to be here. If everything goes as planned, Bethany and Devon will be able to come home with us later that week. The adoption won't be finalized yet, but they will be living here until it is. I'm so excited!"

"Oh, Vicki, I'm thrilled for you and David. Are you going to redecorate the bedrooms before they come home?"

"A little. Maybe paint the walls and buy child-sized beds in place of those queen and king ones."

Lucy laughed, "I can only stay for a few days, but I know how to handle a paint roller.

Would it be okay if I bring Jarrod with me? He needs some diversion from his unpredictable life for a while. Until Annie can come home, he's been shuffled here and there. And he keeps reminding me that Cal promised to take him for a ride on a real horse if he ever made it to Texas."

"Sure, bring him along." Vicki hesitated before offering to call Cal. Her last words to him hadn't been especially kind. "Do you want me to tell Cal when you'll be here so he can make sure he's available for Jarrod's ride?"

Lucy thought about saying yes, but told herself that was the coward's way out. "No, I'll try calling him. Maybe that's the excuse I need." She briefly explained the events of the days since Cal flew home. "You'll be happy to know your Uncle Leon was here. We've talked. He's flying back to Denver today."

Vicki was pleased to hear her mother and her uncle had talked, at least. She also knew she owed Cal Frasier an apology for the way she spoke to him.

Lucy dialed Cal's number. "Cal? This is Lucy. Listen, before you hang up on me, I want to let you know I'll be bringing Jarrod with me when I come for the adoption hearing on October 20th. He talks about you telling him he could ride a horse when we come. I wanted to make sure you would be there if you're still willing to take him riding."

Cal didn't answer immediately. He had asked himself a hundred times how he would respond if Lucy called, but every angry thought he had left him as soon as he heard her voice.

"Thank you for letting me know the date. Of course, I'll be happy to put Jarrod on a horse." He continued, "I'm glad you called. It's good to hear your voice again, Lucy."

"Cal, I wasn't sure you would take my call. I can't tell you how sorry I am for my hateful words to you. I know I have a lot of explaining to do, but I would rather say the things I want to say in person. It can't all be erased with a simple, "I'm sorry." For now, I would like to ask for your forgiveness."

"Of course. You were understandably upset. Perhaps we can talk about a lot of things when you're here in a few weeks."

"Yes, perhaps we can." Before she ended the call, she said quietly, "Cal, I miss you."

CHAPTER 22

LIFE FOR THE NEWSOME family was beginning to return to normal or, possibly, a *new normal*. Paul returned to his job and had an interview with a different company. Lynne was planning to do some tutoring from their home and homeschool Annie when she was released from the hospital so she wouldn't fall behind.

Lucy tried to stop and see Annie every day, even if only for a few minutes. Now that she didn't need someone with her every waking minute, she quickly got bored. The doctor talked about sending her home soon. Her speech and cognitive skills were improving rapidly. Unfortunately, the leg would take much longer. Paul made arrangements for a hospital bed to be delivered and set up in the family room. She would need a wheelchair, also. The present cast would eventually be replaced with a bent-knee cast. They were told these types of multiple breaks can take months to heal, but Annie's youth was in her favor.

* * *

"Ben, what are your plans for today?" Cal asked.

"I'm going to check the fences in the south quarter. One of the guys said he saw places they needed restrung. Why?"

"Just wondering if you'd like some company."

"Sure." Ben sensed there was more to his father's request than fixing fences.

They rode in silence for a long time, enjoying the fall weather and each other's company.

"I'm not going to beat around the bush, Ben. Do you and Candy love each other?"

Ben was a bit taken aback, as his father wasn't usually quite that candid.

"Yes, I guess we do."

"There is no guessing about it. You either know in your heart you love someone or you don't. Do you have doubts?"

Ben thought for a bit, and then answered. "No. I have no doubts. I do love her and would like nothing better than to spend the rest of my life with her."

"What are you waiting for? Ask her. You're 29 years old, Ben. Time is not going to wait for you. If you're worried about where you'll live, the ranch house is big enough for two families. You and Candy can raise a family right there. It will all be yours one day, anyway. If you want it, that is. Maybe I'm presuming too much."

"Dad, you know I love this place, always have. What about Jackie and Samantha?"

"Your sisters are taken care of, Ben. They don't have any interest in the ranch and won't have a stake in it. I was recently reminded of what happened when another young man had to assume responsibility of a large property. He wasn't prepared for it and ended up losing it. I don't want that to happen to you. I have absolute confidence in your abilities, but I also want you to know you can ask for advice or help any time you need it."

"I don't understand, exactly. Why are we having this conversation? This is still your spread. Are you planning on leaving or is there some health issue I don't know about?" Ben asked.

Cal laughed. "No, I'm healthy as a horse but maybe I'm feeling a little 'old' lately and I want to make the necessary arrangements while I still know my own name."

"Since we're being candid...I think you're feeling old because you don't have Lucy in your life. I wish I could go back to the cookout and tell my sisters to go home before they started talking. If you love Lucy, Dad, then take the advice you gave me a few minutes ago. Ask her to marry you. Who cares how long you've known her or your ages or the stupid things the girls were saying about her? I could tell how she affected you the first time I met her. You seemed the happiest I've seen you since Mom died."

"I was happy, Ben. She seems to have a hold on me and even though I've been trying to get on with life, she is in my thoughts every minute of every day. I can hardly wait for her to visit in October for a few days. But then what? She's going to get on that plane and fly out of my life again. I don't want a long distance affair. I don't want to see her every few months. I want her in my arms where I can hold her every day. If that's TMI as they say, I'm sorry."

Ben smiled. "No, I understand but unfortunately, I don't have the answer. You and Lucy will have to work that out."

*　*　*

"Phoebe, how would you like a short vacation? It's not the cruise we talked about, but a few days in Texas, and I will still pick up the tab if you agree to go. I'm taking Jarrod, too."

"Well, let me think...late October in Chicago or nice temperatures in Texas—which should I choose?"

"I should warn you, it may involve a little painting if we help Vicki with the kids' bedrooms."

"I wield a mean paintbrush. Count me in."

Lucy filled her in on the details and purchased the tickets for the three of them.

* * *

Lucy asked Catherine to have lunch with her. "I want your opinion, Catherine. I trust it implicitly. Do you think I should replace James or eliminate his position permanently?"

Catherine didn't have to think about her answer. "It appears to me James didn't do much for the past six months, anyway."

"That's true. The thing I don't like is that almost all of the meetings James had to attend, are in the evening. I guess I'm feeling my age or something, but I'm not wild about being in the city late in the evenings anymore. A few years ago, there were times I would stay overnight in my office when it got too late to drive home. I felt safe due to the security at our building, but it doesn't appeal to me on a regular basis anymore. I'll have to give this matter some more thought."

"Can I ask you something, Louisa? What happened to your 'cowboy' friend? I know I only met him once, but he seemed like the perfect match for you. And I have to say, he was very handsome, too."

"Oh Catherine, you're blushing again just talking about Cal. He does seem like the perfect guy, but we've hit a bit of a snag in our relationship. I don't know if we can overcome it or not. I truly hope so, because I think I love him. Is that possible after knowing someone for such a short time?"

"Absolutely. My husband and I only had five dates when he asked me to marry him. Sometimes, you just know, y'know?"

* * *

Cal met Jerry for lunch. "I'm buying your lunch, Jerry, so you can answer a legal question for me."

"I should have known there was an ulterior motive when you offered to buy," Jerry said.

"How do I go about deeding a very small portion of the ranch to someone?"

"Now, or after you die?"

"I want to do it as soon as possible."

"You may need the expertise of a real estate lawyer. It could be a simple process, but sometimes 'simple' is a relative term."

* * *

The day for departure finally arrived. Jarrod was talking non-stop. He was wearing the hat Cal sent and was beyond excited. The flight was uneventful, and Jarrod even took a short nap.

Vicki was supposed to be coming to get them, but Lucy didn't see her car as she scanned the vehicles in the pick-up lane. Then she noticed a familiar car, and her heart nearly jumped out of her chest. Cal stepped out of his car and stowed the bags in the trunk, with Jarrod chattering to him all the while.

She was a bit nervous about seeing Cal again, even though their phone conversation had gone well.

"Well, Mr. Frasier, what are you doing here? Did my daughter coerce you to come get us?"

"She didn't have to ask me. I asked her. I didn't think I could wait another minute to see you, Lucy. Welcome to Texas."

Cal grabbed her around the waist, pulled her toward him and kissed her. The kiss lasted long enough that the cars in the line behind his were honking their horns.

"Ahem." Phoebe cleared her throat in mock dismay. "Do you greet all visitors that way?"

Cal smiled. "No, only certain ones. You must be Phoebe. I've heard a lot about you and heard your voice on speaker phone," he teased. "But I've never had the pleasure of meeting you."

Phoebe shook his hand and crawled into the back seat with Jarrod, who was busily buckling himself into his seat belt.

"Are we going riding today, Cal?"

"We're going to let your grandma and Aunt Vicki set the schedule, okay Pardner?"

As Lucy looked at him, she thought she would prefer to spend every minute of all three days with him and let everyone else keep a schedule of some kind.

* * *

"Hi, Candy. Can you come out to the ranch this evening? I want to show you a special place I found today while Dad and I were out repairing fences. Wear your jeans and boots."

Candy giggled. "OK. What are you planning, Ben? I don't have to go rock climbing, do I?"

"No. It may have something to do with a rock, but I promise, no rock climbing. I'll see you around 7."

CHAPTER 23

CAL DROPPED THEM at Vicki's house, carried their bags inside and told Jarrod he would be waiting for him when it was time to ride.

"Jarrod," Vicki cried as he ran to her outstretched arms. "I haven't seen you for almost a year. It was last Thanksgiving."

"I know. Do you know Annie got hit and she has a cast on and she gets to sleep on a bed in the living room?"

Vicki was laughing. "Oh my, Jarrod, you can talk, can't you?" She turned to Phoebe. "Hi Phoebe. It's nice to see you again, too. Mom says you're willing to paint a few walls while you're here?'

"Anything you say, Vicki. I am so happy for you and David being able to adopt two little ones."

"Did I hear my name?" David said as he came into the kitchen. "I do appreciate your help with the painting. We don't expect you to slave away all the time you're here. We thought maybe you'd get bored."

"Let me tell you, David, if you had seen the kiss that cowboy planted on your mother-in-law when he saw her at the airport, I don't think she's going to be bored. And Jarrod's going riding, so I guess you're stuck with me. Just hand me a brush."

Vicki looked at Lucy. "Did Jarrod see that?"

"No. He was already in the car, but what if he had? He's certainly seen his dad kiss his mom."

"But...you're his grandma," she protested.

Lucy rolled her eyes, partly because she knew Vicki hated it when she did that. "Grandmas deserve kisses, too. What time is the meeting tomorrow?"

"It's scheduled for 10 a.m., but Jerry suggested we arrive at least a half hour early. It shouldn't take too long. As I understand it, it's simply a required legal formality."

"So, show me the colors you picked out for the kids' rooms."

Vicki showed them three colors: green, yellow and pink.

"Why three? Are you painting three of the rooms? Please tell me you aren't using pink for the room where I sleep."

"No. Pink is for Bethany's room, green is for Devon's and yellow is for the baby's room."

It took a minute for that to sink in. Speechless, Lucy just stared at both of them.

"A baby? You're having a baby?" Suddenly she remembered all the "feeling sick" mornings when she was here earlier. "How did that happen?"

David answered, "Since you have two children, we were hoping *you* could tell us how that happened." Lucy laughed, and there were hugs all around.

"That's why I asked for your help with the painting. I'm not supposed to breathe the fumes."

"I have an idea, Vicki," Lucy suggested. "Why don't you and David go to a hotel after the meeting tomorrow, and we'll get these rooms painted. It's the perfect answer. You two have a nice respite, and we can accomplish something. I'll ask Cal to help."

"Oh boy. Now we know how much painting will get done," Phoebe interjected.

* * *

After a late lunch, Lucy drove David's car to take Jarrod riding. As she drove, she wondered if she could do this. It would be the first time she had seen her childhood home in 23 years. Had she let go of her feelings of animosity for Leon and Cal, or were they just being buried and subdued for now? She would know soon enough. She took a deep breath and stopped at the end of the long, winding drive that led to the main house. Seeing the metal sign with a large scrolled 'B' on it over the end of the drive gave her pause. There used to be a wooden sign that said, "Yellow Rose Ranch" hanging there. This would be harder than she anticipated. So many memories came flooding back; she closed her eyes and hoped they would disappear. Finally, she steeled herself to drive to the ranch house.

Cal came out to meet them. He looked at Lucy, knowing this would be extremely difficult. "Are you OK with this? I could have picked him up."

"I have to conquer my fear sometime. I'd rather do it with you here than on my own."

Some things looked the same, but the house had a different roof and a new porch that ran all the way across the front of the two adjoining houses, there was a guesthouse added behind the main house, and the patio had been enlarged and embellished with flagstone floor and a built-in grill. There were also new stables, but the circle drive was the same. She smiled when she saw the rose bushes her grandma loved, still in the front flowerbeds. They weren't blooming at this time of year, but she instinctively knew they were yellow.

"Can we ride around your whole ranch, Cal? I want to see all of it," Jarrod asked excitedly.

"I think you'll have to come back another time if you want to see all of it, Jarrod. Let's just get you on a horse, first. I have one saddled I think will work for you. Her name is Nell."

Cal lifted Jarrod onto Nell's back. His feet barely reached the stirrups even though Cal had shortened them. He walked the horse around the yard for a while. When he was sure Jarrod could stay on, Cal mounted Cutter, and taking Nell's reins, he led her down a path, with Jarrod hanging on tightly and grinning from ear to ear.

* * *

Ben emerged from the house and found Lucy sitting on a porch swing waiting for the riders to return.

He sat down beside her. "Hi, Lucy. It's nice to see you. I'm glad you're here. Maybe now Dad will smile again."

She acknowledged the thought and smiled, too.

"He really cares for you, and I want you to know, I am not like my sisters. I don't care about any of that stuff they dug up about your past. I think you are the best thing that could happen to Dad, and I give your relationship my blessing, for what it's worth."

Warning bells were going off in Lucy's head. *What stuff,* she wondered. *Might as well ask, Lucy. There have been enough secrets.*

"Tell me, Ben, what did your sisters find in my memorable past?" She laughed, trying to put him at ease.

"I'm not totally certain what they were talking about, but something about a trial and a trust fund. Oh, and you'll love this one. They tried to convince Dad you were still married to some guy."

Lucy said nothing, she just nodded her head, letting Ben know she heard him. Perhaps he would continue to think that was an absurd idea. They continued to talk about other things, until the *horsemen* came riding back.

Jarrod was still smiling and now he had the reins in his hands, although Cal was close enough to grab them if he needed to. Lucy helped Jarrod slide off Nell. "Did you have a good time, Sweetie?" she asked.

"Yes, Grammy. Do you think Dad would let me have a horse?"

Lucy laughed at her little rider. "I don't think we can have horses in our neighborhood, Jarrod. But there are places near where we live where we could go riding some time."

Jarrod frowned. "No, I think I just want to ride Cal's horses if I can't have one of my own."

*   *   *

Before they left for Vicki's house, Lucy asked Cal, "Got any big plans for tomorrow? If not, how do you feel about painting some bedrooms at Vicki's after the meeting?" She explained the reason, still finding it hard to believe.

Cal agreed and said he would try to find a few other people to help so it would only take a couple of hours.

*   *   *

After dinner, Phoebe wanted to watch a favorite television series, Jarrod was worn out and already asleep, and David had a meeting at church. Lucy took her cup of coffee to the deck where Vicki joined her.

"Vicki, I can't find the words to tell you how ecstatic I am about the adoption and the new baby. You are going to have your hands full, but this is what you have always wanted—a house full of children. God has certainly blessed you and David." She paused as if lost in thought. "Your father would be proud of you."

Vicki looked at her mother. Lucy rarely, if ever, mentioned her and Paul's father. Paul was 9 and she was 7 when he died. He was sick for several years before that, so they didn't have many fun childhood memories of him.

Maybe it's time to let go of all the old hurts and forgive you, too, John, Lucy thought.

*   *   *

The meeting started on time, which Jerry seemed to think was a miracle of some magnitude. Everything was in order, and Lucy was asked some questions and a lot of papers were shuffled back and forth. It was decided the children would start coming to the house for visits twice a week while the final details were accomplished.

The sun was shining when they left the courthouse. David took Vicki and their bags and immediately left for the hotel.

* * *

Cal showed up at the house with Ben and Candy in tow. "Look who I found, and they said they love to paint."

When Jerry found out about the paint party he volunteered to help after going home to change clothes.

Lucy introduced Phoebe to Jerry and sent them to the green room. Ben and Candy took the pink room, and she and Cal started in the yellow room. David had graciously taped all the woodwork and put drop cloths on the floors, so it was merely a matter of spreading paint on the walls and not on themselves. Jarrod helped by amusing himself with the super hero action figures he brought along.

The afternoon went by quickly. The rooms were finished, and no one was covered in paint. They opened the windows to allow the fumes to escape.

Jerry ordered pizza delivered. They sat on the living room floor and ate it because Jarrod wanted to have a picnic.

Lucy had met Candy only briefly, once prior to today. She was a pretty young woman with thick red hair and freckles. She was very quiet but seemed infatuated with Ben.

"This probably isn't the time to say this—I mean sitting on the floor eating pizza, but Candy and I have something to tell you," Ben said as he looked around at everyone.

Ben took her left hand and held it out for them to see. A gorgeous diamond sparkled on her ring finger. She seemed embarrassed, and her freckles stood out even more. "I asked her to be my wife, and she said yes."

Everyone clapped and congratulated them.

A little later, Cal and Ben walked out to the deck together for a minute.

"When did this happen?" Cal asked. "Weren't we discussing this only a few days ago?"

Ben smiled and put his arm around Cal's shoulders. "You always taught me to do what you said, Dad. So I did. Now it's your turn to take my advice."

CHAPTER 24

LUCY WOKE THE NEXT morning, stumbled to the kitchen and made a pot of coffee. While she was drinking it, Phoebe joined her.

"You know, pull-out couches are not all they're advertised to be or maybe my bones like the familiarity of my own bed," she observed, rubbing her back.

Lucy agreed. "I didn't think about sleeping arrangements before we came. I thought you could have the fifth bedroom and Jarrod could sleep on the couch."

They took their coffee to the family room. "What would you like to do today, Phoebe? Tomorrow we leave, so let's do something fun today."

Phoebe grinned sheepishly. "You and I can see each other any time, right? Jerry asked me to join him today for lunch and then some sightseeing."

Lucy stared at her friend and then they both collapsed in laughter. "Well, you go, Phoebe-girl. Have a good time. Knock his socks off with your sparkling wit and sense of humor."

* * *

Before everyone left yesterday, Candy had asked Jarrod if he would like to go with her and Ben to see a small rodeo that was in the area. He wanted to as long as he could wear his hat. Ben assured him everybody would have their cowboy hats on. He rushed through breakfast to get ready.

After he left with them, Lucy stretched like a lazy cat and considered her options. She could pretend she didn't know about the things Cal's daughters told him. She could not see Cal today so she wouldn't have to tell him anything or she could tell him the entire sordid story. *What should I do, Lord? I need your guidance in this matter. You know Cal's heart, and if these revelations bother him, it would be best to know it now instead of later. I don't know if I can handle one more happening in my life. Annie's accident, firing James, Leon showing up, David and Vicki pregnant, visiting the Yellow Rose after all these years; I'm exhausted emotionally. I'm bringing it all to you, Jesus. If this is the time to share, please be with me and give me strength.*

Cal called to see what everyone was doing. She explained they had all left for the day.

"Do you think it's wise for me to come there? We both know what happened the last time we were left alone."

Lucy started laughing and couldn't stop. When she regained her composure, she said, "Do you know how silly that sounded? We aren't a couple of lovesick teenagers. Please come over. I will try to keep my hands to myself."

*   *   *

Before Cal left home, he called Paul. "Paul, I apologize for calling you at work. Can you talk for a minute?"

"Sure. I'm actually driving and have you on speaker. Go ahead."

"I feel foolish asking this question, but I need to know and can't ask your mother, for various reasons. Did Lucy divorce her second husband? I know it was a short marriage, but she did actually get a divorce, correct?"

"Yes. Yes, I'm sure she did. I mean, why wouldn't she? Yes, Cal, I am absolutely certain she is a free woman."

"Thank you, Paul. Please don't mention that I called to ask, okay?"

"Sure thing. Tell Jarrod we miss him."

*   *   *

Cal found Lucy curled up on the couch in the family room. She was staring out the windows that surrounded half the room.

He sat down next to her and immediately kissed her. She pulled away. In mock seriousness, she said, "Now don't you start with that kissin' stuff, young man, or I'll have to sit on my hands to keep 'em off of you. You know, we have no self-control."

They poured another cup of coffee and moved to the deck. The weather was clear and cool, perfect for sitting outside.

Now's the time, Lucy.

"Cal, when I spoke to Ben yesterday, he told me your daughters did some investigating into my past."

Cal interrupted her. "It doesn't matter, Lucy. Not one thing matters, except I love you. There, I said it. Can I kiss you now?"

She stood up. "I love you, too, and that's why it does matter, Cal. Ever since the night you told me I needed God and then Leon told me the same thing, I have resumed my relationship with him. I know he never left; I did. But I also know I need him in my life and I am trying, with his help, to give my anger and doubts and past hurts to him."

Cal stood, put his arms around her and held her tightly. "Lucy, you can say whatever you feel you need to. I will be right here." They sat on the glider.

"This is a long involved tale, so please bear with me. I have to start back when I was in college and fell in love with a young man named John Newsome. We grew up in totally different environments. My life was probably considered sheltered, while John was a street-wise kid. He had some minor brushes with the law, tried a few drugs and drank, a lot. While I didn't participate, those things made him very exciting, forbidden fruit to me. We dated, I graduated and we got married."

"John painted cars for a living and was very good at it. A year after we were married, Barry, a former acquaintance of his, called and said he had a great business opportunity for him. Barry had a building and all the equipment just waiting for John to take over. The only negative part was that it was in Chicago, Illinois."

"Grandma and Grandpa tried to tell us not to go, but of course, we knew everything, so off we went. It was just as Barry said it would be—a great set-up. Barry even found an accountant for the business, so John wouldn't have to worry about figuring all the different taxes and payroll."

"A year after we arrived, Paul was born. John was making a good income. We bought a nice little house, and two years later, Victoria made an appearance. Life seemed idyllic. The business was doing so well, John wanted to expand and look for a bigger building. That's when Barry told him he could not move and would never be able to. It seems John's business was a front for Barry's racketeering activities: money laundering, drugs, guns, you name it. You're probably wondering how John could work there every day and not suspect anything. If you're as shrewd as Barry was, it can be accomplished."

"When John got sick the first time, he was afraid he would die and not be able to provide for me and the children. He struck a deal with the devil. Barry was to create a trust with a substantial amount of money, put it in my name and not tell me until John died. The deal was that John would continue the business as long as he could and never turn Barry over to the police. John's bargaining chip was that he wasn't afraid of Barry's threats or of going to prison himself. He was a dying man; what did he have to lose? But he had everything to gain for his family. Barry did as John asked. Is that called honor among thieves? I don't know, but shortly before he died, John told me about the entire situation. He made me promise I would use the trust money for the kids and me to survive."

"I didn't want to use illegal money, but I became desperate. The medical bills, the funeral—I had to keep my children safe. I was angrier at John than I was at Barry. How dare he leave us in this mess? I sold the house, took the money from the trust and bought a house in Batavia that was scheduled for demolition. It was structurally sound, but some investors believed it was more profitable to level an older home and build a new one on the property. I had enough left to make a few renovations. Now the kids and I at least had a home no one could take from us. I got a job in an office, using my business degree skills. I saved every penny I could and when another older home was going to be torn down, I took out a mortgage on it and did the same thing I did with mine. Then I sold it for a profit. I may have been *flipping houses* before that was even a term."

Lucy opened a soda, took a deep breath and continued. "I reasoned if I could make money on individual houses, why not try a group of houses? When Grandma and Grandpa died, Leon and I each inherited half of the ranch and half of a portfolio of cash and investments. I took my half of the portfolio and started my business."

"I won't bore you with all the details of the business, but suffice it to say, I got tough, quickly. If there's anything some men hate more than a successful man, it's a successful, intelligent woman. I was offered bribes of every sort: money, vacations, stocks, government appointments, sleepovers, cruises. You name it, it was offered. I'm not implying every agency I had to deal with was corrupt, but there were enough people to make it necessary never to let your guard down and always watch your back. I became very shrewd at discovering who were the good guys and who were the bad guys, and they all knew it."

"A high-ranking official came to me asking me to bend the regulations, just a little, to ensure the city would make a huge profit off some low-income housing. The people who lived in those houses had enough problems. They didn't deserve substandard materials and shoddy workmanship on top of it. I refused and turned the information over to the State's Attorney, whom I knew to be an honest person. I received death threats, some of my on-site equipment was destroyed, all kinds of things. Finally, he coerced Barry...yes, Barry...into testifying that I knew about the trust, where the money had come from and that I still used it. Part of that, of course, was true. I did know where it came from when I used it. This information about me was supposed to convince the State's Attorney to dismiss the case because I took bribes also and could not be believed."

"It took two years of court proceedings, testifying and trying to hang on to my contracts and my business reputation, but in the end, I was exonerated. Barry and the official were indicted on all charges. Barry died in prison; I don't know what happened to Councilman Gordon. He's probably still serving time somewhere. It was big news at the time, which is why I'm sure it is still online and your daughters had no trouble finding it."

"So, Marshal, that's my story, and I'm stickin' to it." She put her head on his shoulder and closed her eyes.

Cal shook his head, trying to absorb what Lucy's world must be like. He couldn't even imagine that kind of pressure on a daily basis. He much preferred stubborn cattle and obstinate horses. He decided not to ask about the divorce. She was tired.

CHAPTER 25

AS THEY WERE PREPARING to leave for the airport, Vicki asked Lucy, "Mom, do you remember Marilyn Wagner? Someone told her you were here earlier this fall. She found me at church and asked about you. She said it had been so long that she probably wouldn't recognize you. I looked for this picture of you and James I still have on my phone from a year ago because it is such a great picture of you. She was impressed." Vicki laughed. "That's what daughters are for, right? Make their moms look as good as possible."

Lucy shook her head and smiled. "I'm happy you're protecting my image, Vicki, but can you use a computer program of some sort to edit James out of it so I don't have to be reminded of him?"

Cal immediately realized it was the picture he saw on Vicki's phone that day at church and mentally kicked himself for thinking the worst.

"Cal, can my sister come the next time Grammy comes to Texas?" Jarrod asked. "She'll have her cast off by then and she can ride on Nell, too. I'll teach her, okay?"

Cal knelt down to Jarrod's level. "That would be wonderful, Jarrod. Tell her to bring her hat. A cowgirl can't ride without a hat, you know."

"I know. I will. Good-bye, Cal." Jarrod put his arms around Cal's neck and gave him a hug. "I'm sure glad you're Grammy's friend."

Jarrod and Phoebe headed to security. Lucy put her arms around Cal's neck. "This Grammy is sure glad you're her friend, too."

Cal started to kiss her. She gave him a feigned surprise look. "Why, Marshal, were you going to kiss me right here in front of all these people?"

"What people?" he asked as he picked her up off the floor a few inches so he could twirl her around. Then he kissed her passionately and whispered, "I don't want you to go."

"I know. But November isn't too far away, and you and Ben and Candy are coming for Thanksgiving, right? Bring Jerry along, Phoebe would like that," she laughed. They parted and she boarded the plane.

"Grammy, are you crying," Jarrod asked.

"Just one little tear, Sweetie. I always cry one tear when I leave Texas."

"Why don't you just move here? Then you'd never have to cry that tear again."

Lucy smiled and ruffled his hair. "Not a bad idea, Jarrod."

* * *

It was bitterly cold. Annie was tired of being in a cast and not being able to do things. Paul was considering a job offer with a company in Oklahoma. Vicki and David sent weekly pictures of Bethany and Devon and of Vicki's growing tummy.

Cal sent a picture of his family gathered for an early Thanksgiving dinner at the ranch. He had convinced his daughters their fears about Lucy were unfounded. Lucy invited them and their families to Illinois for Thanksgiving, also, but they declined saying it was too expensive for that many people to fly.

Lucy was working overtime. She had not hired anyone to replace James, which made it hard to cover all the bases. She would interview some people after the first of the year. Right now, she just had to get through a few more weeks until she could put her arms around Cal again.

*　*　*

Cal bought his ticket so he could arrive a few days early and surprise Lucy. He wanted a couple of days alone with her before everyone else arrived.

Lucy was mentally making a list of preparations for Thanksgiving dinner and where everyone would sleep. Paul and Lynne offered a bedroom if it was needed. It was going to be a marvelous time. She could hardly wait. A couple more days of working and she could stay home for a week or more. She drove into the city on Monday morning. She worked at the office until noon and then drove to the site to see progress inside the houses.

She met Phoebe for a late lunch. "Shouldn't you be heading home?" Phoebe asked.

"I will. But I have one more meeting tonight. You know how government works. They're all trying to finish business before the holiday."

"Be careful, Lucy. I worry about you being out so late in the dark."

"I'll be careful, Phoebe. If it runs too late, I'll sleep at the office like I used to do. See you for dinner on Thursday."

*　*　*

The meeting did run late, very late. She had some papers she needed to take back to the office anyway, so she'd take them now, stay over and go home early tomorrow when it was daylight.

"Mrs. Crowder, what are you doing here so late?" Frank asked as she blew in the door.

"I had a late meeting, Frank. I'm sure glad to see you're still here. I'm going to stay over, OK? I don't want you to worry if you don't see me come back down."

"I'll be here all night. I switched with Cory for the night."

Lucy left the elevator and unlocked the office. She put her briefcase on a chair and her purse on the desk. She decided to make a cup of tea; maybe it would warm her a bit. She sat at the desk, warming her hands on the mug. She thought she heard a noise behind her but dismissed it. Then she felt the cold end of a revolver on the left side of her neck.

Stay calm, Lucy, she told herself.

The person holding the gun came around to her left side where she could see him.

"So, you're the dark shadow hanging over my shoulder in my dreams," Lucy commented.

"Aww, you been dreamin' about me, Lucy? How touching."

"I should have said nightmare, not dream."

"You won't have so many smart answers when you're dead."

He had obviously been drinking, which could be to her advantage if he didn't get careless with that gun.

"So, fill me in. How, exactly, are you planning on killing me?"

"I'm not going to kill you—you are. Poor Louisa, when they investigate your business accounts and find them empty, they will understand why you took your own life. Hand me your phone."

She handed it to him, and he promptly smashed it. Then he tore the cords out of the security cameras. "Put your hands behind your back."

As he started to tie her wrists, Lucy asked, "Don't you think the police are going to question how I could kill myself with my hands tied behind my back?"

He grunted and let go of her hands. "You're right. You're going to need your hands to pull the trigger on this gun and end your life."

* * *

Frank was looking at the wiring on the console. Funny, he thought. It all looked like it was in place. He wondered why the cameras in Mrs. Crowder's office went offline. Maybe she unplugged them since she was going to spend the night.

* * *

When Cal got off the plane, he called Paul. "Have you heard from your mother?" he asked.

"No. But she may be working late. If she did, she sometimes decides to stay in the city."

"She's not answering her cell phone. It seems to be turned off. Does that seem strange?"

Paul was becoming concerned. "Yes, very strange. She never turns her phone off. She calls it her lifeline."

"I'm going to take a cab to her office, just to check. I'm sure everything is okay, Paul. I didn't mean to worry you."

Cal wasn't at all sure everything was okay.

* * *

"If I'm going to die, do you mind telling me why?"

"Why?" he laughed derisively. "Because you ruined my life, that's why."

"Just how did I do that?"

"I did everything they told me to. I wined and dined you. I told you how beautiful you were. I comforted you when you were lonely…and still, it wasn't enough. You tried divorcing me. But that didn't work, did it?"

"Derek, you stole everything that wasn't locked down…jewelry, cash, credit cards, bank accounts."

Derek leered at her, "Yes, but not all of it, huh, Lucy? No. You thought you would be clever, hiding some of 'our' money where I couldn't get to it."

"Our money?" Lucy asked incredulously. "You didn't earn a dime of it. You just spent it. All that wining and dining was on my charge cards."

There's a missing piece here, Lucy. Think, think.

She tried reasoning with him. "You do realize most men don't kill their wives because they think they hid money from them, right?"

Derek shook his head, as if to clear the cobwebs from his memory. "You mean there's something the all-knowing Louisa doesn't know?"

* * *

Cal urged the cab driver to hurry.

* * *

"You sent my father to jail. Councilman Gordon…remember him? I was supposed to help him get some dirt on you. That's why I married you. You hid everything and then you testified against him. You ruined his reputation and his life…and mine."

Councilman Gordon was Derek's father? How had she missed that fact?

"That wimp, James, was supposed to get the hidden account numbers for me, and you ruined that too," Derek whined.

Derek continued talking, "I'm out of money, but not for long, huh? I'm sure a judge will determine that the grieving widower should be compensated, especially since his recently departed wife was so wealthy."

Lucy's mind was working overtime. She glanced at her purse on the desk. If she could get him to hit her, she might have a chance. He had an abusive streak when he'd been drinking.

"Derek, you won't get away with this. You were never smart enough to tie your shoes, let alone plan my murder and then make it look like a suicide."

"Really? Is that what you think, Louisa? Why did you marry me? For the fun between the sheets?" he grinned.

Now was her opportunity; she knew how to make him angry enough to hit her.

Lucy let her lip curl in disgust. "You must be kidding. You were never any good in that department either."

Lucy knew it was coming and braced for it. He hit her hard across the face. The ring he was wearing tore into her cheek. The metallic taste of blood almost made her gag as she felt it running out the corner of her mouth. That was good; it was exactly what she wanted to happen. She started to reach for her purse.

"Keep your hands on the desk," he hissed.

"Can I get a tissue out of my purse? You know, this is a $200 blouse, and I don't want bloodstains on it. Besides, Derek, you know I always like to look nice. I want it clean for when they zip me into a body bag."

He grinned at the thought and motioned for her to go ahead and get the tissue. She reached into her purse.

* * *

"Frank, bring the key to Lucy's office...now." Cal bounded up the stairs. He didn't have time to wait for the elevator.

*   *   *

Derek walked toward the end of the room, still waving the gun around. He turned toward her.

"You know, Louisa, I always admired you. You seemed to have it all: money, prestige, looks, success and brains. You thought you were so smart. You enjoyed winning, in business and in your life. You thought you could win at everything, didn't you? You even used to brag about how you could beat me at poker. Well, not this time, Louisa. This time, I'm the one holding the winning hand."

"You may think so, Derek…but I have pocket aces."

She pulled the trigger and Derek stumbled backward, ending up on the floor, with his back against the doorframe. He dropped the gun and was clutching his shoulder while a crimson stain was growing on the front of his shirt. His eyes were wide with disbelief at what just happened.

Cal reached the door just as he heard the explosion of a revolver. Frank unlocked the door, and they both crashed into the room.

Lucy was sitting at the desk with her hand still inside her purse. The left side of her face was bruised and bleeding with a trickle of blood running down her chin. At the end of the room, obviously shot in the shoulder, was a man he had never seen before.

She looked at Cal then jerked her head toward the man on the floor, "Meet Derek Crowder, my husband."

CHAPTER 26

CAL WAS HAVING TROUBLE absorbing the scene in front of him. It was surreal, like a dream or a scene from a movie. It definitely wasn't a dream though. There was a man with a bullet hole through him writhing in agony and bleeding profusely.

The police and paramedics arrived. Frank had called them as soon as he and Cal entered the room.

Lucy stood up and watched as the man she shot was loaded onto a stretcher and taken from the room. The look on her face told Cal it wouldn't take much for her to unload the remaining four bullets into him.

"Mrs. Crowder?" the policeman asked.

Lucy nodded slowly, and then shook her head to erase the scene that had just played out in her office.

"Mrs. Crowder, I'm Sergeant Ames and this is my partner, Detective Ellis. I need to ask you some questions, but first I'd like you to tell me where the gun is."

Lucy pointed to her purse, "Inside my bag."

She seemed to have regained her composure. "Go ahead and ask your questions."

"Okay. Let's start with this: can you tell me who the man was that was just taken out of here?"

"Yes, of course. His name is Derek Crowder. He is still my husband although I've been trying to divorce him for years. If you check, there's a warrant for his arrest, somewhere. The State's Attorney should have record of it."

"Did you invite him here tonight?"

Lucy sighed. "No. I don't know how he snuck in, probably when Frank and Cory changed places at the security desk in the lobby. He did have a key to my office when we were first married. I assume he kept it for just such an occasion. I kept thinking I needed to ask for my locks to be changed, but I never got around to it."

"Is this weapon registered in your name?" he asked as he pulled it from her purse.

"It is, Sergeant."

Cal moved to Lucy's side and placed his arm protectively around her waist.

"And who are you?"

"Calvin Frasier."

Addressing Lucy, he said, "Can you tell me what happened?"

"Derek came here to kill me and make it look like a suicide. I shot him. You'll likely find the bullet lodged in the doorframe behind where you found him. I have the entire encounter on tape."

Detective Ellis looked at the torn wires from the security cameras and shook his head. "These won't do you any good."

"I had a friend install a second security system a few months ago."

Cal smiled. Of course, that's what Anthony was doing in her office.

Sergeant Ames looked at the two people in front of him. They seemed like an unlikely pair. She was dressed in business clothes: black boots, long leather skirt and silk blouse while Mr. Frasier was dressed in a long suede coat. His cowboy boots and Western hat made it appear that he just rode in from the prairie. The way he was looking at her, he was definitely more than a friend. Was this a love triangle gone wrong?

Detective Ellis touched the hole in the side of Lucy's purse, prompting her to comment, "Terrible thing to do to a new Coach purse, huh?"

After using Lucy's computer to review the tapes, Sergeant Ames told them they were free to go. He would have to keep her gun until all the reports were filed. He complimented her on her cool thinking under pressure.

"I get loads of practice in my line of work, Sergeant."

"You may need to testify. Someone will let you know if it's necessary."

"Lucy, are you ready for me to take you home or should I call Paul and tell him we're staying in town tonight?" Cal asked. "We can go home in the morning."

"There is absolutely nothing I would like better than staying in a hotel with you, but we probably should go home."

* * *

As Cal drove Lucy's car through the darkened streets, he wondered about this woman sitting next to him. A few hours ago, a man was threatening to kill her. He didn't see any tears or fright or remorse. She seemed to take it all in stride. In fact, the hole she put in her expensive purse seemed to upset her more than the hole she put in a man. Perhaps it would hit her later. He called Paul and told him all was well and they were on their way home. If Lucy wanted to share the details in the morning, that was up to her.

Cal unlocked the front door and took her coat. She removed her boots and tossed them in a corner.

"Can I get you a cup of coffee or something, Lucy?"

"There's a bottle of whiskey in the top cupboard. Neat, please."

When Cal handed her the glass he asked, "You do realize you shot a man tonight, right?"

"Grandpa always told me there were more two-legged snakes than the ones that slithered on their bellies. But he said either one would die if your aim was good enough. My aim wasn't good enough tonight."

She downed the whiskey and went to the kitchen to refill her glass.

"Would you like to talk about it?"

"Which part?" she shouted. "The fact that your daughters were right and I am still married or the fact I didn't trust you enough to tell you or maybe the fact I really, really missed the boat when I didn't check far enough on Derek or that I was so pathetically lonesome, I fell for his BS or maybe that he had to be bribed to date me to begin with? Which one should we discuss first, Cal?"

She slammed the glass down on the counter so hard, it shattered. She looked at it, turned and walked into the spare bedroom located off the living room.

Cal cleaned up the broken glass and returned to the couch. He sat with his head in his hands for a while.

* * *

What now, Lord? What do I do? I love this woman and I truly believe you brought her into my life, but I'm confused about the next step. I want to take her home with me and protect her forever. Please guide me.

* * *

He went to the bedroom. Lucy was curled up on top of the covers, still dressed. He lay down next to her, placed his arm around her waist and said, "I will never let go of you, Lucy. We'll work through this together. I love you." He didn't know if she heard him or not but he held her all night while she slept.

Lucy heard him and silent tears slid down her cheeks until she fell asleep.

* * *

The doorbell rang. Someone knocked incessantly. Lucy stirred. Cal went to answer the door. Paul was standing there looking at him.

"Come in, Paul."

"I tried calling Mom's phone. There is still no answer. Is she here?"

"Yes, she's sleeping," Cal said quietly.

"What's going on? What happened last night? Is she okay?" His eyes fell on the bottle of whiskey still on the counter. He looked questioningly at Cal.

"There was an intruder at her office when she returned from a meeting. He threatened her. She shot him, and I brought her home. That's our evening in a nutshell."

Paul looked at him as though he were speaking a foreign language. He sat down on a kitchen stool, trying to comprehend what Cal had just said.

"She shot him? Is he dead? Who was it and why was he there?"

"He isn't dead. It was Derek Crowder. He had been drinking and was seeking revenge for something."

Lucy walked out of the bedroom. "Good morning, Paul."

The left side of her face was swollen and had turned purple, her lip was split and she had bloodstains on her blouse.

"Oh my gosh, Mom! What did he do to you?" Paul put his hands on her shoulders while he checked her face. "Is he going to jail, I hope?"

"If I had time to aim a little better, he'd be on a slab at the morgue instead of going to jail. I'm going upstairs to take a shower. Please don't tell Annie and Jarrod. I will tell them I fell or something. And Paul, if you talk to your sister, don't mention this. She doesn't need any stress right now. I will tell her sometime."

She picked up her boots from where she'd tossed them last night and proceeded up the stairs. Lucy looked at her reflection in the mirror; she gingerly touched her face and lip and winced. She would put some essential oil on after she showered. It would speed up the healing process.

Lucy's swollen lip curled in disgust as she thought, *the ironic thing is the hole in your cheek was caused by a ring Derek probably bought with your money.*

She unbuttoned her blouse, looked at the bloodstains for a moment, and then dropped it in the trash. *I wish I could throw pieces of my life in the trash as easily as that.*

* * *

After Lucy left the room, Paul said, "You know, I used to give her grief about carrying that gun all the time, but I'm sure glad she had it last night."

Cal nodded in agreement, "Yeah, me too. I was glad she had it the day we went riding after we first met. She saved my life by shooting a rattlesnake. She told me maybe I would save her life one day. I keep thinking I should have been there to save her last night, but I wasn't."

"Cal, you didn't know what was going on. How could you have been there? You should not feel any guilt over this."

"Paul, the only way I know to protect her is to get her out of here and take her to Texas with me."

"You would certainly have my blessing for that, Cal, but she is probably the most independent woman I know. She loves Texas, but I don't know if she would leave her business. As hazardous as it gets sometimes, I think she gets an adrenaline rush when she wins or overcomes some seemingly insurmountable obstacle."

CHAPTER 27

BEFORE SHE SHOWERED, Lucy found a phone she had owned previously. It didn't have all the bells and whistles as the one that was destroyed, but it would allow her to be connected. She would have it activated. Perhaps her contacts could be switched even though the other one was beyond repair.

As the hot water ran over her body, her thoughts wandered. *Beyond repair...interesting phrase. How many relationships in my life have been damaged beyond repair? Too many, Lord, too many. Even my relationship with you isn't what I would like it to be. Please don't let it be beyond repair, Jesus.*

* * *

When she came down, Paul had left. Cal was having a cup of coffee and reading the newspaper. He looked up as she walked into the room.

"Cal, we need to talk."

"It's okay, Lucy. We don't have to discuss anything right now. Give it some time."

"No. I think the time is now, Cal. I need to tell you why I'm not divorced. I should have told you when I first met you. It wasn't fair to let you believe I was divorced. I really didn't expect you to find out the way you did, but..." She shrugged her shoulders. "God has a way of forcing our hand sometimes."

She poured a cup of coffee and sat down across from him. "I filed for divorce as soon as Derek left and took everything with him. At that time, there wasn't a no-fault divorce law on the books. The existing law stipulated a waiting period of several years. My next step was to have him declared legally dead. That used to take seven years, also, but it doesn't any more. I was required to post notices anywhere he might see them. That was a total waste of time; I had no idea where he was. He might have left for Mexico for all I knew. He certainly absconded with enough money to live comfortably for a very long time."

She pushed her coffee cup away. She couldn't drink without making her lip hurt. "When the law was amended, it made it possible to have someone declared legally dead even if they had only been missing for a few weeks. I thought I was home free. However, it is up to the discretion of the presiding judge if there is enough evidence that the person is dead. The judge always decided perhaps Derek was still alive, even though no one had seen him for years. It became a legal nightmare. The only positive aspect of his coming back last night is the fact that now there is definite proof he's alive and I can file for the no-fault divorce."

"There's another reason I believe he didn't want the divorce to be final. In the state of Illinois, the percentage of spousal support is based on how many years you've been married. I guess when he was drunk enough, it sounded like a good idea to kill me instead and get all of the spoils instead of some measly percentage."

"You're kidding me. You mean he could still want you to support him with spousal support?"

"I'm fairly certain the security tape the police have and his going to prison will squelch any kind of support. However, I never count on anything when it comes to the legal system."

"Lucy, I wanted to say this at a candlelight dinner, not in your kitchen, but it doesn't matter. When your legal entanglements are over, will you marry me? I don't know how we'll work out the long distance details or my ranching and your business or any of that. I only know I don't want to live without you. I love you and need you. I want to spend the rest of my life with you."

Lucy looked at this handsome man sitting across from her. *Was he asking because of what he witnessed last night? She knew he would protect her and take care of her. Did she need someone to take care of her? Did she want someone to take care of her? Would she end up damaging this relationship beyond repair, also? Would his daughters ever accept her? Cal loved her and asked nothing of her but to love him in return. Did she love him enough to make this work…whatever that meant?*

"Yes, Calvin Benson Frasier, I will marry you," she said quietly.

He came to her and cupped her chin in his hand. He kissed her very gently so he didn't hurt her split lip.

* * *

Lucy dialed Anthony's number. "I'd like to take you to lunch, Anthony. Can we meet at Folger's today at 11 o'clock?"

When she entered the café, he yelled, "Hey Louisa, shouldn't you be home stuffing a turkey for tomorrow?"

"You haven't heard about my lack of culinary skills, have you?" she laughed, then winced as smiling made her face hurt.

"I wanted to thank you for your security camera installation skills. They probably kept me from being charged with attempted murder on Monday evening." She gave him the shortened version of what happened.

Anthony always knew Lucy carried a revolver. He was happy she had it and knew how to use it. He looked at her bruised face and frowned, and then he spoke very seriously. "Louisa, get out of this business. You've paid your debt." When she looked at him questioningly, he continued. "I know about you being accused of using the trust money even though you knew where it came from. You've been trying to absolve your guilt over that by helping low-income families with the best housing possible. As I said, you've paid your debt. Sell your business, move to Texas and marry your cowboy. Life is too short to mess around."

"Anthony, you never told me you were a psychiatrist, too."

"Yep, all kinds of degrees," he laughed. "I've been wanting to tell you this but haven't found a good time. I'm going to retire after the next two projects are finished. This cold weather is getting to me. Emma and I have a place in Florida, and we're going to enjoy the sunshine. I could never work for another person after working for you, so it's time to go...for both of us."

* * *

Thursday morning was cold and windy. Paul drove to O'Hare to pick up Ben, Candy and Jerry. Cal rode along to speak to Paul.

"I've asked your mother to marry me, Paul. I know I'm doing this backwards, asking her first and then asking you and Vicki for your blessing, but the time seemed right on Tuesday morning. I don't know when or how we will work out the details, but we will. Right now, all I know is she said yes. I'd appreciate it if you wouldn't tell anyone until I can talk to Vicki, too."

"Congratulations, Cal. I'm more than happy to give you and Mom my blessing, even though you don't need it. I have every confidence you will find a way to make it all work. God has a plan, and I'm happy to watch it unfold."

When everyone arrived, including Phoebe, there were introductions all around. Paul and Lynne had never met Ben, Candy or Jerry.

Cal briefly explained the bruises on Lucy's face and the situation in her office on Monday evening. Phoebe already knew, but the others found the entire scenario almost unbelievable.

Everyone pitched in to help with the preparations. Candy had a sweet quiet nature and she definitely knew her way around a kitchen. She was in charge of telling everyone else what to do. Jarrod helped set the table and Annie placed napkins and the good silver on the table as she wheeled around the dining room. When everyone was seated, Lucy asked Paul to say the blessing.

"Heavenly Father, we thank and praise you for the many blessings you shower upon us. Thank you for Annie's healing, for protecting Mom and for safe travel. Thank you for friends and loved ones to share time with. Bless this food and our lives, today and every day. In Jesus' name, Amen."

Dinner was declared a success. As usual, on holidays, everyone ate more than they should.

"Ben, have you and Candy set a date for your wedding?" Jerry asked.

Candy smiled shyly. "Yes, right before Christmas. It will be just family and a few friends, so it shouldn't interfere with anyone's holiday plans."

They discussed world events, weather predictions, Paul's interview and Annie's recovery.

* * *

After everyone was gone on Friday and the house was empty again, Lucy sat in the living room with Cal. He had his long legs stretched out on the couch and his head on her lap. She ran her fingers through his hair.

"Any ideas how we're going to make this work, Marshal?"

"A few. I don't want to take your life away from you, Lucy. I would be willing to give Ben full control of the ranch and move here if that's what it takes for me to have you in my life."

Lucy smiled, remembering her comments to Vicki, months ago. *One of her requirements for a man was that he had to be willing to leave everything to be with her. The question was would she be willing to do the same thing? Could she tell him she would leave everything behind and join him at the ranch?*

They sat in silence for a long time. Finally, Lucy spoke.

"You won't have to do that, Cal. Your life is in Texas. Mine was there at one time. Now it will be again."

CHAPTER 28

BEFORE SHE LEFT, Candy asked Lucy if she would be her witness at the small wedding she and Ben were planning. "I'm honored Candy, but are you certain? I'm sure you have a good friend you would like to stand up with you?"

"My best friend is expecting a baby that week, and I have no sisters, only four brothers. Ben's dad is going to be his best man so I thought maybe you would like to stand up with me."

"Of course, I will.

* * *

Cal asked Lucy if she would like to go to dinner before he flew back to Texas on Saturday. He told her it was a "dress-up" affair and laughed at her expression.

He was wearing a suit and waiting in the living room when she came down the stairs. She was wearing silver heels and a long turquoise dress that had a side slit in the skirt. She had her hair twisted in a bun on the top of her head. She had made an extra effort to hide the remaining bruising on her face. The diamond necklace she was wearing sparkled in the light. Cal thought all she needed was a tiara and she would have looked like a princess. When he voiced that thought out loud, she laughingly reminded him she was a bit too old to be a princess, but she'd settle for queen. He gave her his hand when she reached the last two steps, and then swept her into his arms. He whispered in her ear, "I have a better idea than going out. Why don't we stay here and dance all night long?"

"That sounds inviting, but I spent too much time getting ready. At my age, it takes a long time to look this good," she teased. "Let's go."

* * *

He drove to an elegant restaurant in downtown Chicago. After dinner, he asked her to dance with him. Lucy was smiling all the while they danced. She had no idea Cal would be a good dancer. As they swayed to a slow dance, she wondered how many other surprises there would be in their lives together.

They hadn't known each other long enough to discover all the little things. This would definitely be an exciting adventure.

When they returned to the table, Cal told her, "I know I asked you to marry me several nights ago, but I'm old-fashioned enough to want to do it right. I asked Paul for his blessing and I called Victoria to get hers. So, I'm going to ask you again. Louisa, will you marry me?"

Without hesitation, Lucy answered, "Yes, Marshal, I would be thrilled to be your wife."

Cal looked down at his calloused hands, then up into Lucy's eyes. He opened a small box and set it in front of her. Nestled in the velvet was a yellow diamond in a rose-shaped setting. He took it out and slipped it on her ring finger. "A yellow rose," Lucy whispered. She reached out to take his face in her hands and kissed him for a very long time.

* * *

She could hardly wait to show Paul and Lynne. They were both excited and pleased by the proposal. Paul told them he had accepted the offer in Oklahoma. They would be putting their house on the market in a few months.

It was always bittersweet when either one of them was boarding a plane. Even though Cal was the one leaving, Lucy felt as though she should be singing the last line to John Denver's song, stating she would be so lonesome she could die.

* * *

She and Vicki spoke nearly every day. The adoption was finalized, and Bethany and Devon were settled in the Marsh household. The baby wasn't due until May, but Vicki definitely had a baby bump showing.

Lucy asked, "The doctor doesn't think you may be having twins, does he?"

"Bite your tongue, Mom. I don't think I could handle four children under the age of 4."

Lucy laughed at the thought of her meticulous, organized daughter with four little ones. It was definitely going to be a fun ride, even with three.

* * *

By the first week in December, Lucy's attorney sent the divorce decree along with the court order for the legal removal of Crowder from her name. Finally, she was free of Derek and every reminder of him.

Lucy was trying to figure out how she was going to accomplish everything that needed to be done in the amount of time she had. There were a million loose ends she needed to tie up before she closed her business permanently in the spring. She found a position for Catherine with a company she trusted to be a good employer. She gave her a substantial bonus for always being her eyes and ears at the office.

She needed to put her house on the market but that could wait until spring. Most buyers with children wouldn't start looking until the school year was over.

Annie was due to lose the cast soon and would be able to accompany her to Texas when she went for Ben and Candy's wedding. She had done no Christmas shopping yet, and it was only a few weeks away. She would not abandon the projects that were already contracted. Anthony agreed to stay until the last section of houses would be completed and ready for occupancy. She would keep her office open until then and travel back and forth.

When she spoke to Cal on the phone, she told him, "Honey, I think we should be able to go to Hawaii on our honeymoon for free, using the frequent flyer miles I'm going to accumulate by spring."

"If you don't mind, Lucy, I have a better plan for our honeymoon."

"You're in charge. I'm leaving this all up to you. We don't have to go anywhere. I would be happy staying at the ranch."

* * *

Cal asked Ben when he came in for dinner, "When you were out today, did you have a chance to check on the project we talked about?"

"Yeah, I did. It's looking good, Dad. I think it will be exactly what you wanted. Sam said you should come by next week; he has a few questions to ask."

* * *

"Okay, Annie, here we go. Are you ready for this big adventure?"

"Yes, Grammy, and I have my hat 'cause Cal told me to bring it."

When they arrived at the airport in Houston, Candy was waiting to pick them up. "Cal and Ben were both loading cattle so I volunteered," she explained.

When they were on the way to Vicki's house, Lucy asked, "Are you ready for your big day, Candy?"

"I'm excited and scared, too, Lucy. I pray I can be the wife Ben needs."

"You are exactly the wife Ben needs, or he wouldn't have fallen head over cowboy boots in love with you."

Annie laughed. "That's funny, Grammy."

Candy noticed the ring on Lucy's finger. Her eyes opened wide but before she could say anything, Lucy put her finger to her lips and shook her head. They both knew what the ring meant but since Lucy and Cal hadn't told anyone yet, she didn't want to explain it to Annie right then.

*   *   *

Candy dropped Lucy and Annie at Vicki's house. Vicki and David hugged Annie until she squealed. Lucy dropped to one knee and spoke to Devon and Bethany, but understood it would take a while for them to be comfortable with these new people in their lives. Annie had lots of questions about Aunt Victoria's round tummy and wanted to know how soon she could hold that baby. She was excited about meeting her new cousins, but all three were a bit shy at first. Annie's bouncy personality took over, and soon they were playing in the family room.

Lucy told Victoria to close her eyes. "I have a surprise for you and David. You can open them now." She held out her hand with the diamond on it.

Vicki had tears in her eyes. "It's beautiful, Mom. I'm sorry I gave you and Cal so much grief. You deserve to be happy, and he certainly seems to make you happy."

David looked at the ring, also. Then he put his arms around Lucy. "It will be the best thing that has happened to you in a long time."

* * *

When the cattle were loaded, Cal went back to the ranch and showered. It was early afternoon when he stopped by and asked Annie if she was ready to go riding. Lucy knew he had to be tired. She suggested they wait until tomorrow.

Cal shook his head, "Nope. Nell's been waiting all day to give Annie a ride. We don't want to disappoint either one of them."

When they arrived, Ben had Nell saddled and ready to go. Cal lifted Annie onto the horse's back and hung on to her. He didn't want to risk injuring that leg again. They walked around the yard, then down the drive to the barn and back.

When they reached the yard in front of the porch, Cal asked, "Lucy, do you want to ride with her? I don't want her to slide off and her leg isn't strong enough to squeeze against the horse. I'm too big for Nell."

Lucy smiled. This would be a sight. She hitched her skirt up so she could swing her leg over and squeezed in behind Annie. Cal handed her the reins. Lucy told Annie, "Okay, Baby, hang on. Here we go."

Lucy took her for a long ride. It felt good to be riding again. Soon she would be able to ride every day if she wanted. She would even work the cattle with Cal some days, if he didn't mind. She knew how to do that, and she was pretty sure she could still rope a calf if she needed to. All those thoughts made her smile. Then she frowned. She also knew she would have to find something to be involved in or some kind of work away from the ranch. She wasn't exactly the Ladies Auxiliary type. If she didn't find a cause, she ran the risk of being bored and restless. She knew herself too well.

When she thought Annie had enough for one day, she headed back to the barn. Cal lifted Annie down and then caught Lucy as she slipped down. He hung on to her, brushed a few stray strands of hair off her face and kissed her. "You look mighty good up there, Miss Lucy."

When they walked up to the porch, Annie whispered to Candy and Ben, "Cal kissed my Grammy. I saw him."

Everyone laughed and Lucy hugged Annie. "Its okay, Annie. Grammy is going to marry Cal, but you can't tell yet. It's a secret, OK?"

She nodded so hard, her curls bounced. Lucy held her hand out to Ben to see the ring. "Your father has excellent taste in diamonds, Ben."

"Yes he does. He had me bring it with me when we came at Thanksgiving. I didn't know when he was going to give it to you but I'm happy to see he did."

* * *

Ben and Candy agreed they wanted a small wedding. It was going to be at the church but only friends and family had been invited. Candy's parents were divorced and living in Massachusetts and California. Neither one would be able to attend. Lucy felt sorry for Candy; her father wouldn't be there to walk her down the aisle, and her brothers weren't making an effort to attend either. It seemed like a strange situation, but if anyone understood unusual family dynamics, it was Lucy.

Jackie and Samantha and their families arrived at the church and were seated in the front row. When Candy's very pregnant girlfriend and her husband got there, Lucy asked if Annie could sit with them. *Oh please, God, don't let her have that baby during the wedding. That would be more than I want to explain to Annie,* Lucy thought.

Candy wore a simple knee-length dress, and Ben looked handsome in a Western-cut sport coat. Lucy was again amazed at how much he resembled Cal. They didn't look exactly alike, but they were nearly the same height and build, and their smiles and mannerisms were much the same.

Lucy stole a glance at Jackie and Samantha. They were both attractive women, at least on the outside, she thought. It didn't matter; she was marrying Cal, not his daughters.

After the ceremony and before dinner, Cal finally had a chance to introduce Lucy to his daughters and their families. Knowing what they knew about each other, it was a bit stiff and awkward. Lucy and Cal agreed she should not wear the ring until he had a chance to talk to the girls. Lucy felt as though she was being scrutinized in every sense of the word, but it was fine with her. She had definitely lived through worse situations and survived.

After dinner, Ben and Candy left for a week-long honeymoon. Nearly everyone else went back to the ranch before heading home. Lucy took the children for a walk as Cal said he wanted to talk with his girls...alone.

CHAPTER 29

CAL ASKED JACKIE and Samantha and their husbands to hear what he had to say before they replied or interrupted.

"I know the last time we were together it was pretty heated. I checked everything you said about Lucy, and we've discussed it all. We have no secrets. You were correct, she was still married, but that also is a long story and has been taken care of."

"I know we haven't known each other very long, but I assure you it is long enough. I have asked her to be my wife, and she said yes. She is giving up a life and home she loves and a business she has built for many years to come here to the ranch and live with me."

"I am not forgetting your mother. We had a very special love, and it won't be replaced by my love for Lucy. Her children's father died also. I am not replacing him. But I also want you to know she is nothing like your mother, so please don't compare them. Your mother was a wonderful homemaker, an outstanding cook and quiet. Lucy was taught to ride, rope, shoot and play poker. And as far as I can tell, she's damned good at all of those things. And, quiet is not a word I would use to describe her. She lives her life with a fierceness I can't describe."

"The ranch house will be hers to do with as she pleases. If she wants to redecorate, I certainly won't stop her. I only mention that because I don't want her to feel as though you will be upset if she changes something."

"Legally, I have taken care of you and your children. Ben and Candy will inherit the ranch after Lucy and I die. Everything I have is hers. I haven't even talked to Lucy about that but I assure you she doesn't need my money. However, I would marry her if she was destitute."

"I love her more than I can tell you. I am asking for your blessing and I pray you will accept the things I told you, and accept her and make her feel welcome, but if you choose not to, I will marry her anyway. She completes me and I don't ever want to live without her. That's all I have to say."

Samantha looked at Cal as though she had never seen him before. "Daddy, I'm sorry I hurt you when I said those things about Lucy. I love you very much and do not want you to be hurt. I saw what happened to you when Mom died. I don't want you to feel like that again…but you're right. You are old enough to know what you're doing."

She looked at Sean, and he nodded. "You have our blessing."

Jackie and Gary agreed. "We want you to be happy, and she certainly seems to make you happy. You have our blessing, too."

Lucy didn't ask Cal what was said at the family meeting, but when she returned with the kids, all four adults congratulated her, and the two girls hugged her.

* * *

Cal came to Batavia to spend Christmas with Lucy and her family. This would be the last Christmas Vicki and Paul would spend in their childhood home. By next Christmas, Vicki and David would have another little one at their house, and Paul and Lynne and the children would be living in Oklahoma. It was a bittersweet time.

They all bundled up and went to church on Christmas Eve. The next morning was total mayhem but so much fun.

As Cal and Lucy sat together on the end of the couch and watched the wrapping paper fly, he rubbed her back and couldn't stop thinking about the difference between last Christmas and this one. Last year he was lonely and depressed. This year he could hardly wait until this woman was his wife. He didn't think he had ever been happier.

The New Year's celebrations came and went. Lucy and Cal agreed they would not try to be together for the end of the year. They spoke on the phone and told each other they would spend every New Year together for the rest of their lives.

* * *

March was the month they chose for their wedding so it would be warm enough to be outside but not extremely hot. It would be at the ranch and informal. Their families, including Leon and his wife, Ginny, and Cal and Lucy's friends would share the day with them. Lucy invited Anthony and his wife and Catherine and her husband. Cal invited the ranch foreman and a few of the ranch hands and their families and Simon and his wife. Ben would be Cal's best man and Phoebe would be Lucy's matron of honor, although she protested that title, saying it made her sound like she was 90. Jeans and boots were acceptable attire. The decision was made to allow the grandchildren to stand with Lucy and Cal if they wanted instead of trying to make them be quiet and sit still.

* * *

There were so many things that needed to be done before March. Lucy spent her time between her office, trying to wrap up loose ends, and home, where she was sorting through years of keepsakes, mementos and useless junk. She did find her Grandma's worn Bible. She held it to her heart and pictured Grandma reading it to her. She made the decision to carry it on her wedding day.

March finally arrived. The weeks before the wedding were a blur of preparations. Even though they had tried to keep it simple, there were still decisions about the food, cake, music, flowers and seating arrangements. Lucy made sure Samantha, Jackie, Candy and Vicki were all involved in the decisions. Lynne was included too, from long distance, using Skype.

Everyone who lived somewhere other than Texas flew in the day before the wedding. Lucy finally got to meet Leon's wife, Ginny, but Cal's sister would not be able to attend.

Lucy told Cal she was sure a "simple" wedding was more work than an elaborate one. Chairs were delivered from a rental store and set in rows on the lawn. Flowers were placed along the walk from the porch to the place where she would meet Cal.

*   *   *

As Phoebe was helping Lucy with her hair, she asked her, "Honey, are you sure this is what you want? There's still time. We can grab a couple of horses and get the heck outta' Dodge."

Lucy laughed at her friend. "Phoebe, you've never ridden a horse in your life. Besides, this is exactly what I want."

Then in a serious voice, Phoebe said, "Lucy, I told you a thousand times to bring a cowboy home, but I believe the cowboy has brought you home." She hugged her. "Be happy, Lucy."

Lucy stepped out of the house wearing jeans, boots, and a lace top. Phoebe had braided baby's breath and tiny yellow roses into her hair. Amy and Annie each held one of her hands and Bethany held on to Annie's hand. Together, they walked her down the "aisle" of the yard. The four boys stood by Cal and Ben, with Gabe hanging on to Cal's leg.

As she walked toward him, Cal thought again how beautiful she was. It seemed he had known her all his life instead of six months.

Lucy never took her eyes off Cal as she walked toward him. She smiled at him. This man caught her attention when he walked into the Long Branch Café last fall, and she never stopped thinking about him since that moment.

They had decided to write their own short vows to say before the usual ones.

Cal began by saying, "You saved my life several months ago, and I intend to make certain you never have a reason to regret doing so. You make my life complete, Lucy. I can't imagine a day without you in it. I will love you forever. Everything I have is yours."

Lucy took his hand and said quietly. "I will never forget the first time I saw you. I think I fell in love with you that night and have been loving you ever since. Your love and patience have changed my life in many ways. You brought me into your arms and back into the arms of my Savior. I will love you forever. Everything I have is yours, including my heart."

"Calvin Benson Frasier, do you take Louisa Mae Henderson Newsome to be your lawfully wedded wife?" Cal didn't hear the rest, he could only look at Lucy and hear his heart beating.

"I do."

"Louisa Mae Henderson Newsome, do you take Calvin Benson Frasier to be your lawfully wedded husband?"

"I do."

They exchanged rings. Cal's was a plain band with an inscription inside. Lucy's matched her engagement ring.

"I now pronounce you man and wife."

Cal put his arms around her, bent her backwards and kissed her so long, the guests were whistling and applauding. Six of the grandchildren were dancing around them. Ben picked Gabe up and was holding him above the mayhem, as all the noise was bothering him.

Paul wrapped his arms around Lucy and whispered in her ear, "God blessed you with a good man, Mom. I want this part of your life to be the best it has ever been."

Lynne hugged her and thanked her for always being there for them over the years.

There were several grills going, and the tables were filled with food.

Everyone tried line dancing, except Vicki. She decided she might wait until the baby was born to try it. Catherine cried and asked Lucy to please stay in touch.

Anthony hugged Lucy and shook hands with Cal. "Take especially good care of this girl, y'hear?"

Leon hugged her and told her he and Ginny would be delighted if she and Cal would ever want to visit them in Denver.

Samantha and Jackie apologized again for their concerns and offered to help with anything Lucy decided to do with the house.

Simon offered to fly them to a destination of their choice for their honeymoon. Cal thanked him but told him he had it taken care of.

As the evening wore down and while everyone was still having a good time, Cal nodded to Ben, who headed to the barn. He returned with a sleek black and white Paint mare with flowers braided into her mane. There was a blanket over her but no saddle. Cal handed the reins to Lucy. "She's all yours, Lucy. You can choose a name for her and ride like the wind."

"She's gorgeous," Lucy said as she stroked the mare's neck. She buried her face in her mane. "Hello Harmony," she said. Then she whispered in Cal's ear, "Thank you, Cal. I love you more every minute, if that's possible."

One of the ranch hands brought Cutter, Cal's big bay quarter horse. They both mounted and rode out of the yard to calls of well wishes.

"Where are you taking me, Marshal?"

"It's a surprise, Lucy. I hope you like it."

They rode without speaking. Finally, they approached the spot where her grandparents were buried and she shot the rattler. The tombstones had been straightened and scrubbed.

The iron fence had been replaced, and all the debris was gone. There was no place for a snake to hide. Lucy sat and looked at it for a while.

Then Cal lifted her down and turned her around. There was a small cabin and a lean-to built on land that had been cleared. There were two wooden rockers on the front porch, waiting invitingly. On a sign above the door, the words, The Yellow Rose, were painted.

Before she could ask, Cal explained. "As my wife, you own half of the entire Benson Ranch, but I had three acres deeded to you, and in the record books it is named The Yellow Rose. I know it won't ever make up for the childhood memories, but it's yours. Maybe some days, you will need a respite from the world. You can come here and relax. But tonight I'm staying with you," he said.

Cal led her inside. It reminded her of the great room in the ranch house, only much smaller. It consisted of one room with a tiny bathroom, a table and two chairs and a bed against one wall. A bouquet of yellow roses sat on the table.

After he put the horses in the lean-to for the night, he joined Lucy on the porch. They sat in the rockers until the sun went down and the stars came out. "Cal, this seems like a dream. Everything that has happened in the last six months is almost more than my mind can accept."

"I know, but if it's a dream, I hope I never wake up." He offered her his hand and they went inside. In the darkened room, he held her and asked, "Now that you're my wife, do you think I know you well enough to call you Lucy Mae?"

She put her hands on his shoulders. As her lips brushed his bare chest, she whispered, "You will by morning, Cowboy."

ABOUT THE AUTHOR

Gloria Doty is a Christian author, freelance writer, blogger and speaker. She has written articles for many magazines. Gloria is a regular contributor to a quarterly devotional, *Hope-Full Living* and to *Ruby for Women*, an online magazine for Christian women. Her non-fiction book, *Not Different Enough*, was published in 2014 and was awarded the Writer of the Year award by the WTP Writer's Conference. It is the transparent telling of the first 30 years of life with her daughter, Kalisha, who has autism, Asperger's and mild intellectual disabilities. Gloria and her sister co-authored *A Bouquet of Devotions*, published in 2015.

Bring a Cowboy Home is her first fiction romance novel. Her love of Texas and the towns included in the book were her inspiration. Gloria has five children and 13 grandchildren. She writes from her home in Fort Wayne, IN.

You can read her stories on her blogs, Getting It Right -- Occasionally and Montage Moments, at www.writingbygloria.com

.

COMING SUMMER 2016
THE SECOND NOVEL IN THE SERIES OF THREE

LOVING A COWBOY

CHAPTER 1

"GRAMMA LUCY, GRAMMA LUCY. Wake up. Grandpa says you are a sleepyhead. Come on."

Lucy opened one eye. Cal's 5-year-old granddaughter had her face 2 inches from hers, nearly touching her nose.

"Amy, why are you up so early? Let Gramma sleep a little longer."

"No-o-o, Gramma. Come on. Grandpa's making monkey pancakes."

Lucy opened both eyes and looked over her shoulder where her husband of two months was supposed to be. No Cal. She sighed, swung her legs over the side of the bed and grabbed her summer robe.

Amy took her hand and pulled her to the kitchen.

"See, Gramma? I told you Grandpa was making monkey pancakes."

Lucy moved closer to the stove where Cal was standing at the griddle with a spatula in his hand and grinning at her.

"Monkey pancakes…really? Are you showing off since we both know I can't make regular pancakes without setting off the smoke alarm?" she asked him.

Cal smiled and continued to use a squeeze bottle to put batter on the griddle in the shape of a monkey's face.

"I'm impressed, Love. Where did you learn to do that?" Lucy asked.

"Pinterest."

Lucy's eyes grew wide and she started laughing. Somehow her 6'4" rugged rancher husband didn't fit her idea of the typical Pinterest person.

Intrigued, she asked, "Where did you hear about Pinterest?"

"I heard Samantha talking about it so I thought I'd check it out. That's when I saw these monkey pancakes. I knew the kids would like 'em. Besides, a guy has to stay on top of things, y'know."

Lucy moved closer to him and rubbed her body lightly against his arm. "You do a good job of that, Cowboy."

Cal winked at her and put another pancake on Amy's plate. Looking at Lucy, he asked, "Why don't you put butter and syrup on that for Amy before you get us both in trouble?"

While she helped Amy, Lucy thought making pancakes was one more thing she would add to the list of information she was learning about this man she loved so much. They had only known each other six months before they were married. There were new things she learned every day, and so far they were all positive.

There was a knock on the door that led to the great room, which was situated between their house and the living quarters on the opposite end of the ranch house. Amy ran to open the door.

"Uncle Ben," she yelled as she jumped up to wrap her arms around his neck. "Come in and have monkey pancakes with me," she begged as she pulled him to the table.

Ben gave Lucy a questioning look.

She shrugged her shoulders. "Just one more of your father's many talents he didn't tell me about before I married him." In a more serious voice, she asked, "How's Candy feeling this morning?"

Ben shook his head. "Not good. She wouldn't even let me make coffee. She said the smell was going to send her back to the bathroom. I tucked her in on the couch, left some crackers and water on the end table, and thought I'd come over here and beg a cup of coffee."

Amy, who listened much too intently to conversations between her mother, Cal's daughter Samantha, and her Aunt

Jackie, piped up. "Is Aunt Candy going to have a baby today, Uncle Ben?"

"No, Sweetie. Not for a long time yet, but she doesn't feel very good this morning."

Satisfied with that answer, she asked, "Do you want some pancakes? Grandpa will make some for you. Won't you, Grandpa?"

Cal put a stack of pancakes in front of Ben, while Lucy poured a cup of coffee for him.

"Thanks, Dad. I have to say I'm impressed with the monkey faces." Ben laughed and continued. "I also came to ask what time you were planning on leaving this morning."

Cal glanced at the mess he had made in the kitchen and told Ben, "Give me an hour, okay?"

Ben, with his mouth full, nodded. "That's good. I'll take Amy to the barn with me to feed the horses and then we'll stop at our house so she can say hello to Candy. Why don't you come get me when you're ready to go?"

Lucy told Cal, "I'll clean up the dishes. My talent in the kitchen lies in the clean-up part of cooking. But I'm going to take a shower and get dressed first." She kissed him lightly on the cheek and left.

Cal watched her go, her lightweight robe not doing a very good job of hiding the strong, supple body under it. *God, I don't know why you blessed me with that woman, but I will thank you every day for the rest of my life,* he thought.

* * *

Lucy stepped out of the shower, wrapped an over-sized towel around her and used a smaller one to dry her hair. As she scrutinized her reflection in the mirror, she touched the few streaks of gray that were mixed in with her dark hair. *Was it time to color it? Would Cal like it better if it were all dark?* Her hand touched the scar on her cheek, an ever-present reminder of a dangerous night when she still lived and worked in Chicago, before she moved back to Texas and married Cal.

In the mirror, she saw Cal come into the bathroom and stand behind her. She turned to him, putting her hands on his chest. "Cal, will you love me when my hair is completely gray and my skin is nothing but wrinkles?"

"Lucy, I will love you no matter what color your hair is, and I don't see any wrinkles and I never will."

She reveled in his answer, then asked, "Where's Amy?"

"Ben took her with him. I'm supposed to find him when I'm ready to leave."

"How soon are you leaving?"

He gently tugged on her towel and let it drop to the floor. "Not for a little while."

* * *

After Cal and Ben left for Houston, Lucy went to find Amy. She knocked softly on Candy's door before opening it a crack to peek inside. Candy smiled and motioned for her to come in. Amy was stretched out on the couch, napping, with her head on Candy's lap.

Lucy laughed. "That's what happens when you get up at the crack of dawn and eat a whole stack of pancakes with syrup. That sugar high bottoms out pretty fast."

"Is that what happened?" Candy said, nodding her head. "I wondered why she was so tired this early in the morning."

"I hope Ben isn't napping on the way to town. He ate a stack of them, too."

Candy smiled and told Lucy, "I feel so bad for Ben. This morning sickness is killing me and making his life miserable, too. This morning I wouldn't even let him make coffee. It should have been over a few months ago. I don't know why it still hits me sometimes."

Lucy looked at her daughter-in-law and remembered feeling like that before she had her daughter, Victoria. Thinking about Vicki, she remembered she needed to call her as soon as she went back to her end of the house.

"I know I'm miserable at this stage of pregnancy, but how is Vicki doing?" Candy asked.

"Truthfully, she's pretty miserable too, but part of that is due to her impatience. She has several weeks before her due date, but you'd think she was a month *overdue*. I'm going to stay at their house with Bethany and Devon when she goes to the hospital and possibly for a few days after she gets home. Having three children under the age of 4 is a bit more than they anticipated when she and David made the decision to adopt. They were thrilled to be able to have two children immediately but never dreamed they would have a baby so soon, too."

"Ben and I wanted to wait a little longer before we started a family, but I guess the Lord had other plans," Candy said as she lovingly ran her hand over her belly.

"I hope you and Ben have a dozen, Candy. This ranch house needs all the bedrooms filled with sweet, noisy munchkins."

Candy looked at her dubiously. "I'm thinking maybe two, Lucy. That's a long way from a dozen, but it might be enough."

Candy stroked Amy's forehead, softly brushing the hair out of her eyes. "Why don't we let Amy sleep, and I'll send her over when she wakes up."

Lucy nodded. "If you feel like any food by lunchtime, I'll bring something over. It won't be nearly as exciting as monkey pancakes, but it will taste good. I promise."

Lucy walked through the great room, thinking, *Maybe I should check Pinterest for a recipe.* Then she laughed out loud. *Calvin Frasier, I love you so much. You never fail to amaze me.*

She found the two plastic tubs she had asked Cal to bring down from an upstairs bedroom. Unless visitors needed a place to spend the night, one of the bedrooms above the great room was used more for storage than as a bedroom. The containers were filled with photographs.

She sat on the floor to look at the photos in the first tub. These were her family albums. She spread them out in front of her. Her great-grandparents looked back at her from a posed sepia-colored print. The subjects in that generation's photos always looked so grim. There was never a glimmer of a smile. The next one was a picture of her beloved grandparents, Ivy and Herman Henderson, who raised her and her brother. They were standing in front of the ranch house. It was the Yellow Rose Ranch at that time. The next photo was of her parents, Albert and Selma. They were smiling. Her mother held her baby brother, Leon, while Lucy was sitting on her father's lap. She looked like she was about 3 years old so Leon would have been 1. That must have been taken a year before her parents were both killed when the small plane her father was piloting exploded in mid-air.

Lucy scrutinized the photo. Did she resemble her mother? No, she didn't think so. She did, however, look like a mirror image of her father. Perhaps that was the reason Grandpa spent so much time teaching her the "boy" things like riding, roping calves, shooting a revolver and playing poker. She reminded him of the son he lost way too soon, and she obviously became a replacement for her father in Grandpa's life.

Well, Grandpa, those skills have stood me in good stead over the years. I'm forever grateful for the things you taught me. Her fingers unconsciously felt for the scar on her cheek.

* * *

Made in the USA
Lexington, KY
31 December 2018